A POINT OF PRIDE

Six years before, Casey had adored one of her father's workmen, Gil Blake. But realising she would just be another notch on his bedhead she'd threatened to get him sacked. Now, with her father about to go bankrupt, he's back and she still loves him. But Gil, clearly no longer a builder's labourer, is still angry and wants revenge: Gil whistles and Casey is obliged to dance to his tune. And the moment she stops, her parents will suffer . . .

LIZ FIELDING

A POINT OF PRIDE

Complete and Unabridged

LINFORD
Leicester

First published in Great Britain in 1993

First Linford Edition
published 2010

British Library CIP Data

Fielding, Liz.
   A point of pride.- -(Linford romance library)
   1. Construction workers- -Fiction.
   2. Love stories. 3. Large type books.
   I. Title II. Series
   823.9'14–dc22

   ISBN 978–1–44480–072–2

Published by
F. A. Thorpe (Publishing)
Anstey, Leicestershire

Set by Words & Graphics Ltd.
Anstey, Leicestershire
Printed and bound in Great Britain by
T. J. International Ltd., Padstow, Cornwall

This book is printed on acid-free paper

1

'Smile, sweetheart . . . this is supposed to be the happiest day of your life.'

Not by one flicker of her lashes did Casey O'Connor acknowledge that she had heard the words murmured by the tall grey-clad figure of Gil Blake, as he took her right hand firmly in his own.

She stared resolutely ahead, her face almost the colour of her exquisitely simple ivory silk dress. The vicar smiled reassuringly and then turned to Gil. The wedding service moved inexorably on.

'I Gilliam Edward Blake take thee Catherine Mary O'Connor . . . ' Gil's firm voice rang firmly through the church, every word clearly heard by the congregation come to witness the shockingly sudden marriage of Casey O'Connor to the tall, tanned stranger who had snatched her from under the very nose of the most eligible bachelor in Melchester.

The minister, satisfied with the groom's response, turned to her. 'I Catherine Mary O'Connor take thee Gilliam . . . ' he prompted.

As she heard the words that would bind them together the temptation to flee was so strong that she was uncertain whether she had in fact stepped back, or if it was just her imagination that Gil's fingers tightened possessively over hers.

She glanced nervously at him from under her lashes. His grey eyes regarded her steadily, but there was no warmth to encourage her response. He was demanding her total surrender.

A dart of anger and an inward promise that he would pay dearly for this moment of triumph lent firmness to her voice as she repeated the words. The slightest tightening of his mouth suggested a smile, and no one could have doubted the sincerity of his words as he placed the ring upon her finger.

'With this ring I thee wed, with my body I thee worship ... ' His mouth curved into a self-mocking smile as he added, 'And with all my worldly goods I thee endow.'

By the time the words, 'I pronounce that they be Man and Wife together,' had been spoken Casey felt so brittle that she thought she might crack.

'Catherine?' Gil murmured, and she turned to face him. The faintest smile touched his eyes. 'I never knew that was your name.'

'Gilliam?' She was unable to match the smile but was determined to equal the light banter in his voice. 'What sort of name is that?'

He lifted one shoulder in the slightest shrug, hesitated for just a moment and then touched his lips to hers. 'It's the name of the man you just married. Don't ever forget it.'

Outside it was all bells and confetti and congratulations. The photographer bullied them into poses and to the onlookers Casey supposed it must have looked like any normal wedding. Then she saw Michael, white-faced and disbelieving, among the old headstones of the churchyard. Comfortable, easy, undemanding Michael. Gil followed her gaze and his mouth hardened into a straight line.

'Enough!' He scowled at the photographer and without warning he swept her up into his arms and carried her up the gravel path to the waiting Rolls. He deposited her, breathless and angry, on the back seat and slammed the door behind him.

'Let's go,' he demanded as the driver turned in surprise. The frustrated photographer was still trying to take pictures of them getting into the car but Gil Blake was not interested in photographs; his sole attention was directed towards his bride. 'Michael Hetherington had his chance, Casey. He didn't take it. Forget him!' Before she could back away his hand had captured her tiny waist and jerked her against him. His mouth descended

4

crushingly upon hers, leaving her in no doubt that he intended to make it his business to see that she forgot.

Mindful of the driver, Casey did not struggle. She sat rigid in his arms, her head desperately fighting her body's urgent need to respond to him. Even as she felt herself begin to weaken, he released her.

'Forget him,' he murmured hoarsely as the car halted before the beautiful rambling old house that was her parents' home.

The suddenness of her wedding had left her mother with little choice but to abandon all idea of what she considered an appropriate wedding reception for her only daughter. Instead she had arranged a small wedding breakfast for family and close friends at her home, and never once had she resisted the need to let Casey know exactly how she felt. Casey's patiently repeated assurance that she was 'not pregnant' only seemed to add insult to injury.

As she toyed with her smoked salmon

Casey noted with a certain grim amusement that her flatmate Charlotte was taking full advantage of her position as bridesmaid to lay siege to Gil's best man. She was no doubt hoping to find out a little more about the man who had appeared from nowhere and swept Casey O'Connor off her feet, marrying her under the nose of a man who had been expected to do just that for more than a year. From her frustrated expression Casey guessed that she wasn't having much success.

It was a relief to escape the air of speculation and retire to the bedroom that had been hers before she left home. Charlotte helped her unfasten the satin buttons and loops at the back of her dress and carefully lifted it over her head.

'Well, love, you make a handsome couple.' Casey made no comment. 'Has he told you where he's taking you on honeymoon?'

Casey tried to speak and found she

had to clear her throat. 'No.'

Charlotte giggled. 'A surprise, eh? Well I'm sure if it was me I wouldn't even notice.' She picked some confetti from Casey's tawny upswept hair and held out her jacket.

Casey checked her appearance in the mirror. The cornflower-blue silk of the simple wrap-around skirt exactly matched the highest-heeled shoes she could find, lifting her five feet ten inches to a height that would still be dwarfed by Gil. It was a luxury she had had to forgo when she went out with Michael. She stroked the long paler blue jacket over her hips. Charlotte handed her the stiffened silk hat that echoed her skirt and she fixed it firmly in place with a hatpin. It brought the deep blue of her eyes startlingly to life. She managed a faint, if slightly mocking smile at her reflection. Everything that was proper.

She had, for one wild desperate moment, been tempted to wear something outrageous. Just as well that the black dress had been consigned to the jumble sale. She had enough to cope with in the shape of Gil Blake. It would be foolish to make him angry before it was absolutely necessary.

A light tap on the door brought her back to the present. Charlotte opened it and Gil, now changed into a dark grey suit with a white shirt and burgundy silk tie, walked, without invitation, into her bedroom. Something she would have to get used to.

Charlotte grinned, mouthed, 'Good luck!' behind his back and ducked out of the room, closing the door discreetly behind her.

Gil's face as he allowed his eyes to absorb every detail of her appearance betrayed no emotion. Then, apparently satisfied, he glanced around the spacious bedroom. His eyes came to rest on the bed with its virginal white frilled lace cover.

'Charming.' He looked up and caught her staring at him. 'I'm afraid it will take you a while to lick your new home into this state.' He almost smiled. 'Not that this particular style will suit me.' He indicated the single bed. 'Just in case you were wondering.' He had made no mention of where they were to live, and she had refused to give him the satisfaction of asking now.

She had only seen him once since he had issued his ultimatum, and the stiff little occasion when she had presented him to her stunned parents had hardly been the moment for intimate chatter. But now their marriage was a fact, and detachment was more difficult.

'Where are . . . we going to live?' The word 'we' had been tricky and Gil knew it.

'I thought you would have asked before.'

'You weren't around to ask,' she reminded him coldly. She turned away deliberately and picked up her bag. 'Besides, it is a matter of supreme indifference to me.'

'In that case, my love, you can wait a little while longer to find out.'

'The longer the better,' she said with a chill-factor of minus five. And it was true. She didn't really care. Annisgarth, the golden stone house on the hill above Melchester, had been sold. She would never live there now, and she had never wanted to live anywhere else.

'We're going there now.'

Casey jerked herself back to reality. 'Where?'

'Home, Mrs Blake.'

Her heart gave a treacherous jerk at the name. 'We're not going . . . ' she forced out the word ' . . . on a honeymoon?'

Gil crossed the space between them and she backed nervously until she felt the bed behind her knees and had to stop or fall back across it. 'You're disappointed?' His hand caught her waist and he pulled her close. He stared down at her, his grey eyes unreadable. 'A honeymoon doesn't need a fancy place, Casey,' he murmured. 'If two people love each other the hard ground of a wood is enough . . . '

She gasped and struck out at him wildly. 'How dare you?' she cried, but, pinioning her arms to her sides, he held her easily.

'Like this. This is how I dare.' And his mouth crushed hers in a punishing kiss. Casey fought him angrily until at last he raised his head to smile lazily at her fury. Finding herself loose, she opened her mouth to protest. The sound never came. And this time the kiss was different. His wide mouth moved on hers, caressing, arousing as his tongue slid along hers. Her body rejected her pride and her determination to resist him, and began to respond, at first tentatively, then with a willing passion that at once shocked and elated her. The ice-cold grip she had kept on her emotions since Gil Blake walked back into her life defrosted under the warmth of his lips.

Breathlessly they parted and for a moment they stared at one another. Then Gil raised one sardonic brow. 'I think I've made my point, don't you, Casey?'

With the certain knowledge that she had made a fool of herself, Casey pulled herself free, and this time there was no resistance.

'Make the most of it,' she spat out fiercely. 'It's the last time you'll trick me like that.'

Cold slate eyes locked on hers. 'Exactly my point. Anywhere would do for the sort of honeymoon you have in mind, wouldn't it?' He turned away and straightened his tie in the mirror. 'I've just invested every hard-earned penny I have in a very shaky company. I could have taken your father to the cleaners, Casey. Made you all suffer.' He stared at her through the mirror. 'But your . . . sacrifice has kept his pride intact.'

'You had a bargain!' she spat at him.

He stood up and turned to her. 'That's to be seen. But there's no spare cash for fancy honeymoons and I'll be needed here to start putting things right. You, Catherine Mary Blake, will have to wait until I've more time.'

Angry colour darkened her cheek-bones. He had guessed her intention and suddenly it didn't seem quite such a simple thing to keep this husband from her bed. Not when he made up his mind to share it, although for now he seemed to accept the situation and she supposed she should be grateful for that reprieve. But it seemed a hollow victory. She blinked back the sudden sting of tears behind her eyelids and fled from the room.

He caught her at the foot of the stairs and linked his arm with hers, pausing as he caught sight of his Jaguar decorated with cans and old boots and balloons.

'I see you've all been busy,' he joked easily to the small crowd, gathered to see them on their way, giving her time to arrange her face in the semblance of a smile.

Her father hugged her. At least he had recovered sufficiently to give her away, and that made her sacrifice bearable.

Her mother handed Casey her bouquet and held her daughter close for a moment. 'Casey . . . ?' Then she shook her head, kissed Casey's cheek and stepped back.

She buried her face in the flowers, drowning in the scent, then Gil opened the car door and with an effort at gaiety Casey smiled, shouted, 'Catch!' and tossed the bouquet to the crowd before quickly ducking into the car before anyone noticed the tears pricking at her lids. Once through the gates she let out a long shuddering sigh and closed her eyes, only to open them almost immediately as Gil brought the car to a halt in the lane.

'Out you get.'

'What? That's my car!' she exclaimed as she saw the little red Metro. 'Who's that?'

The driver slid from behind the wheel and surrendered the keys to Gil, who opened the boot of the Jaguar and removed her honeymoon bag, placing it in the back of the red car.

He then gave his own car keys to the driver, together with a banknote. 'That should cover the clean-up job. Thanks, Steve.'

'My pleasure, Gil. Any time,' he said, allowing a curious glance at the bewildered bride.

'Only once, I hope.'

'Oh, sure,' he laughed as he climbed into the larger car, adjusting the seat to his shorter legs.

Gil turned back to Casey. 'Did you want to drive through the town like that?' Her confusion seemed to amuse him.

'No,' she retorted, angrily. 'But how . . . ?'

'Your father was most helpful. Besides, the car is due back at the hire company today. Steve will clean it and take it back for me.'

'Hire company!'

Gil grinned across the top of the little car. 'You didn't actually think it belonged to me, did you?' She made no answer. Of course she'd thought it was his car. With a small cold spot of fear in her stomach she opened the passenger door of the Metro and got in, carefully fastening her seat belt. If he had deceived her about the car, what else was fake? Except, of course, that he had never told her that it was his. Like an idiot she had just assumed it was.

He was a lot closer to her in this car. Even with the seat pushed right back he filled the driver's space and seemed to overflow into hers. She leaned as close to the door as possible, trying to avoid contact with him, but his shoulder brushed against hers whenever he changed gear.

They headed in silence towards the town, skirting the centre and taking the turning towards North Town. Gil drove through several side-streets, dodging the Saturday cars parked in the narrow streets, and pulled up outside a small terraced house.

'Welcome home, Mrs Blake.'

She twitched nervously at the sound of her new name. 'What is this place?' she demanded.

'Twenty-two, Ladysmith Terrace. Our new home. Or, more precisely, your new home. It's always been mine.'

She turned and looked at the faded and blistered front door boasting the number twenty-two. There was one sash window, the glass in need of cleaning, the interior shielded from the street by a net curtain that might once have been white. Appalled, she turned on him. 'You expect me to live here?' she demanded in horror.

'Why not? I was born here. My mother and father lived here. Until recently my aunt Peggy still lived here.'

Casey swallowed. 'And what happened to them all?'

His eyes went blank. 'My father died in an accident on a building site when I was ten years old and my mother never took much care of herself after that.'

'I'm sorry.'

He turned to her. 'Peggy raised me,

but now she's gone to live with her daughter in Birmingham.'

'Who could blame her? And she's left you her house.' She stared around her in dismay.

'No. It's my house. I bought it for my mother as soon as I made a bit of money.'

'And this is where we're going to live?' No honeymoon. No car. No proper house to live in. 'Tell me, Gil. Before I get out of the car and go into Twenty-two, Ladysmith Terrace. Have I been the object of an elaborate hoax?'

'Hoax?' he asked. 'In what way a hoax?'

Casey could see the white lines etched down his cheeks and knew that he was angry, but she was beyond caring. 'You understand me perfectly well. You demanded me in return for rescuing my father's company from bankruptcy.'

'I have. O'Connor Construction is safe, but I've pledged every penny I had to do it.' He gripped the steering-wheel until his knuckles turned white. 'Including the deeds to this house. No less than your father did, in fact . . . ' he bared his teeth in a parody of a smile ' . . . and at least you know the situation. A courtesy, I believe, that Jim O'Connor never showed your mother.'

'How do you know all this?' she demanded, her cheeks flushed.

'I made it my business to know. I'm sorry if you kidded yourself that I was some sort of nabob.' He relented. 'The company is as safe as I can make it. There will be no redundancies and no bankruptcy. In twelve months' time O'Connor Construction will be an accountant's delight.' She let out a breath she had not been aware of holding. 'That was the deal, Casey. I didn't promise a dream house, or a limousine. If there was a hoax, don't blame me for it. You dreamed it up yourself.'

It was true, Casey realised. She had avoided contact with Gil since he had made his outrageous demands and her father's collapse had forced her to accede to them. It had been a point of pride. Perhaps she would have done better to court his company and find out exactly what the situation was. At least she wouldn't have fooled herself quite so thoroughly.

She sat twisting the gold band on her left hand. It felt heavy and uncomfortable. Like a shackle.

Satisfied that he had made his point, Gil went on, 'If you behave yourself and don't get carried away with the housekeeping money, I might be able to afford one of the houses on the new estate in a few months' time.' Casey stared at him in disbelief. 'One of the small ones,' he added, as an afterthought.

'No, thank you. I'd rather live here. At least no one I know is likely to see what I've come to.' She opened the door and swung her legs out on to the pavement to discover that several people were watching with open interest.

'Hello, Snowy. You look nice,' a voice called from across the road. 'Are you going to live there?'

Casey turned with a start and saw a smile, quickly hidden, cross Gil's face. It hadn't taken very long for her secret to be found out. 'Hello, Amy,' she said brightly. 'Yes, we'll be neighbours.' It was one of her Brownies. She realised now that the street name was vaguely familiar. Several of the girls lived in Ladysmith Terrace. Well, at least she wouldn't have far to go on Saturday mornings.

'Snowy?' Gil enquired as he slipped the key into the lock.

'Snowy Owl.' He was clearly puzzled. 'Amy's a Brownie,' she explained.

'A Brownie?' He shook his head in disbelief. 'You run a Brownie Pack? Do you wear one of those little brown tea cosies?'

'Don't be ridiculous,' she snapped.

He swung the door open. 'Ready?' Without waiting for an answer, he swept her off her feet and carried her through the doorway, kicking it shut behind him. For a moment he leaned against it, holding her close to his chest, and Casey could feel his heart beating steadily against her. His body through the thin cloth of her suit was warm and comforting. And she needed to be comforted. Needed someone to put his arms around her and tell her that it would all be better in the morning.

'It doesn't have to be war, Casey,' he murmured.

The sudden knock at the door made them both jump. Gil set her down on her feet, and opened it.

'Is Snowy there?' It was Amy.

Casey went to the door. 'Yes, Amy,' she said, a little unsteadily.

'Mum sent you this.' The child held out a bright yellow polyanthus in a pot, her eyes glued to Gil.

'How lovely. What a kind thought. Will you come in?'

'No. Mum said I mustn't stop. But she said if you want anything she's at number six.'

22

'Well, I'll pop down and see her in a day or two. But thank her for me.'

'OK. Bye.' She watched the child run down the street and then turned back to Gil, but he seemed to have lost interest in her. She placed the plant on the hearth, noticing the dust that lay thickly on the tiles.

'I'm sorry about that.'

He shrugged, the faintest of smiles behind his eyes. 'Are you? Rather timely, I would have thought. The kitchen's through there. Why don't you put the kettle on while I get your bag?'

'Damn!' Casey tore the wide-brimmed hat from her head and threw it on to a chair. In the kitchen she found the kettle. Why had she apologised? Her hand was trembling as she struggled to turn on the old-fashioned tap, which was stiff and squeaky, and the pipes began to clang. The kettle half filled, she placed it on the ancient gas stove and hunted for some matches. She broke three in her trembling fingers before she could get the flame to the gas. It hissed fiercely as she looked around for a teapot and some cups.

There wasn't far to look and she found them on shelves hidden behind a green gingham curtain. She ran a finger along the shelf. At least it was clean there and she started guiltily as Gil appeared in the doorway.

'Found everything?'

'Tea, milk? Is there a fridge?' she asked sharply.

'In the scullery. Through there.' He opened what she had assumed was the back door and she walked into the cool of a long narrow scullery. A modern fridge-freezer took up the entire far wall and she opened the door and produced a pint of milk. 'There's not much here.'

'I've been too busy to shop. And I'm sure you'd prefer to stock your own larder.'

'I can hardly wait,' she said wryly. 'Don't forget to leave me some housekeeping money. Not too much of course.'

He ignored her sarcasm. 'The kettle's

almost boiling. The tea is kept in this cupboard.' He handed her a caddy and their fingers touched inadvertently. She withdrew as if burned and the caddy fell to the floor, spilling the tea.

'I'm . . . '

'Casey . . . '

They both started to speak at once and then stopped, blue and grey eyes locking momentarily before Gil made a move towards her.

'I saw a jar of coffee in there,' Casey said, quickly retreating to the scullery.

Gil stood for a moment then shrugged. 'The dustpan is under the sink.' He turned and walked into the living-room and stretched out in an armchair. Casey ignored the mess on the floor.

'Here's your coffee,' she said, banging it down on the table beside him. 'Perhaps you'd like to show me around while it cools. It clearly isn't going to take very long.'

Gil rose. 'True. We'll have to think of something else to pass the time.' Casey backed away with a rapidity that brought a chuckle to Gil's lips.

They started at the top, a sloping-roofed attic room with a stair that came up through the floor. It was a dusty storeroom, long unused. Casey went over to the dormer window and rubbed at the glass with her hand. She could see across the roof-tops to a small park. 'This could be pretty,' she said, turning away from the window.

'You'll forgive me if I think you have a lively imagination. Come on.' Down one floor there were two doors. Gil opened the first door. 'This used to be my room,' he said. 'Rather different from the ivory tower you were brought up in.' It was a small square room with a bookshelf and a wardrobe. Nothing else. Casey bent and examined the books on the shelf. They were old, and the book plates declared them to be Sunday School prizes. 'These weren't yours,' Casey said.

'Aunt Peggy's,' he confirmed, 'and my father's. But I've read them all. Very instructive. Mostly about people who received their just deserts.' He turned and crossed the landing. 'This is our bedroom.' The bedroom suite had been wonderful when it was new. Probably when the house was built. Two large wardrobes and a vast walnut dressing-table filled the walls. Her suitcases and boxes, collected by van from her flat the day before, took up most of the remaining floor space. The bed, freshly made with clean white sheets and a thick old-fashioned rose eiderdown, sagged slightly in the middle. But the headboard was high and elaborate and Casey walked across to examine it more closely. She rubbed her hand over the carving and felt the comforting spirit of all the women who had loved, given birth and died in the room reach out to her.

'Perhaps we'd better get a new bed . . . ' Gil started.

'Can we afford it?'

Gil regarded her with amusement. 'Not really. Just a new mattress, then.

I've always loved this bed.'

'It's a style that's coming back. It's probably worth holding on to. Where's the bathroom?'

'That's the interior decorator speaking. Your father told me you did the show houses for him.'

'Yes. I have a retainer and . . . ' His use of the past tense suddenly penetrated. 'Did?'

'I won't be giving anyone extravagant retainers. That sort of work will go out to tender.' He shrugged. 'Of course, you can bid if you wish. That is,' he added politely, 'unless you have a contract? I don't remember seeing one.'

Casey could hardly believe her ears. She had always done the show houses for her father, as well as commissions for private houses. She took enormous pride in her work. 'Of course I don't have a contract. Why should I?'

He hooked a finger under her chin and tilted her head up so that she was forced to look him in the eyes. 'Because, Catherine Mary Blake, that's business. You always have a contract, and you always read the small print. Remember that; it saves a lot of disappointment. Now, I believe you wanted to see the bathroom.'

He took her hand firmly in his and with growing bewilderment she followed him back down the stairs, through the kitchen and scullery and out into a small yard where he finally allowed her to snatch her hand away. Hanging against the wall was a long galvanised bungalow bath.

'We take this into the kitchen in the summer,' Gil said with a sly smile. 'But in the winter we put it in front of the fire. It's very cosy.'

Casey felt the colour heating her cheeks. 'You're not serious,' she said finally.

'Why shouldn't I be serious?'

'It's positively . . . medieval!'

'As recent as that? Well, I'm sure you'll be relieved to know that there's a lavatory with a washbasin leading off the scullery.'

'Really?' she asked defiantly. 'And does it flush?'

Angry colour darkened along his cheekbones. 'Don't bank on it,' he snapped. Casey let out a startled cry as he grabbed her wrist and, turning back into the house, he dragged her after him. She tried to pull free, but his grip only tightened and at the foot of the stairs he seized her around the waist, pushed back the door and carried her, yelling and frantically drumming her high sharp heels into his shins, up to the front bedroom, where he dumped her unceremoniously upon the big walnut bed.

'I have had enough condescension from your family for one day, Casey Blake. Your father thinks he's doing me a favour allowing me to buy him out of debt, and your mother with a face like a sepulchre . . . has she any idea how close she came to losing everything, including her house? You're my wife for richer and poorer. If this is as poor as you get you can consider yourself lucky.

I've known worse. Much worse.' He threw the elegant grey jacket on to the floor and ripped off his tie.

'Gil!' she pleaded. 'Don't. There's no need for this.' He ignored her and she came to her senses a moment too late. She rolled sideways as he joined her on the bed, but he reached out and grabbed a handful of her jacket. Frantically, Casey released the buttons and tried to wriggle free, but by then it was too late. His arm was around her waist and he held her easily despite her struggles. With his free hand he flicked the single button of her skirt. Reduced to flimsy cream satin and lace underwear, she began to beat furiously against his shoulders.

'I will not . . . Gil . . . Let me go!' Oblivious of her fists beating at him and her desperate pleading, he pinned her to the bed with one hand while he stripped away her remaining garments.

'Do you think I don't know what you planned, Casey? Did you think you could keep me away from you? You did it once, but now you're my wife and this time, by God, I'll have you.' His voice was harsh and thick with arousal from their struggles.

As she stared up into eyes dark with desire, Casey suddenly became still. It was a pointless undignified struggle and she had been a fool ever to think she could keep him at bay. And perhaps, she thought, as she felt the rough hair of his chest against her breasts, and the stirring of an unfamiliar longing sweeping over her, she didn't really want to. It was pride that was keeping her stiff with resistance.

It was a moment before he realised that she had stopped fighting him. 'Casey?' he murmured softly.

It was only pride that made her turn her head away. 'Go on, Gil. Get it over with.'

White-faced, he drew back as if stung. 'Get it over with?' His lips curled back in contempt. 'How very appealing. About as appealing as making love to a dead fish.'

32

'I don't think love has very much to do with this, do you?'

He groaned, swung his legs from the bed and sat with his back to her, his face in his hands. 'Oh, lord. What have I done?'

Casey stared at the ceiling, fairly certain that an answer wasn't required.

The bed heaved as Gil rose and flung open a wardrobe door, and when he stood over her once more he was wearing jeans and a sweatshirt. 'My apologies, Casey,' he said coldly. 'I lost control, I didn't mean to and I promise you it won't happen again. When you've decided that you want to be a proper wife you must tell me.'

'Hell will freeze over before that happens!' she swore, and meant it.

'As soon as that?' He raised his hand across his heart and sketched a half-mocking little bow. 'Far more than I deserve, I'm sure.' The door opened and she heard him clatter down the stairs. She flinched as the front door slammed behind him.

She waited for what seemed a very long time, but he didn't return. Finally she burrowed under the covers and gave way to the tears that ran silently down her cheeks, splashing on to the old rose eiderdown.

She wondered how many other women had cried under its comfort. Surely none of them because she had too much pride to admit she loved the man she had married. But it was difficult when it was a business arrangement and love was not on the agenda.

She lay in the big bed for a long time before sleep came. Tired as she was, her mind would not settle. Again and again it went over the events of the last month and Gil's cold-blooded ultimatum.

2

Casey had taken a day off work and was sorting clothes for the Brownie jumble sale when the phone rang.

'Casey O'Connor,' she said, flopping down in an armchair. There was a silence. 'Hello?'

'Hello, Casey O'Connor. How are you?' Casey jerked upright, rigid at the sound of a voice she recognised but couldn't, wouldn't quite believe.

'Who is this?'

'I think you know who it is, Casey.'

It was her turn to be silent. It couldn't be him. It was as if thinking about him had conjured him up from the ether. And yet the surge of excitement pounding round her veins assured her that it was.

'Gil?' Her heart was beating anyhow up in her throat and she didn't know what she wanted the answer to be.

'That wasn't so difficult, was it? I've booked a table for one o'clock at the Old Bell.' A little pause. 'I trust you will be free.'

'I . . .'

'Good. I'll see you then.' A click and the line went dead. She drew a long shuddering breath. That hadn't been an invitation, it had been an order. She sat stubbornly in the chair, her fists clenched. Well, she wouldn't go. She wouldn't. Casey glanced at her watch. It was just past twelve o'clock. He hadn't given her much time, hadn't even waited for her answer.

But then he always had been sure of himself, she thought, remembering the first time he had asked her to meet him for a drink. He had waited patiently as she had hesitated, drawn irresistibly to his brawny, rugged, altogether masculine figure, but knowing that her mother would desperately disapprove of her seeing one of her father's workmen, no matter how attractive. There had been a contemptuous twist to his mouth as he had watched her wavering, sensing that she was afraid to say yes, knowing that she wanted to say it.

Well, not this time. She'd leave him sitting there, by the fireplace at the Bell, glancing at his watch, waiting. Except, she thought furiously, he wouldn't wait. She'd tried keeping him waiting once before, in a desperate bid to gain the upper hand in a relationship that had begun to spin giddily out of control. On that occasion, by the time she had arrived he had gone.

She leapt to her feet and flew to the wardrobe, mentally discarding the grey suit even as she reached for it. Not the grey. Not for Gil. Her hand hovered over the black silk jersey dress that she had bought months ago on impulse and never worn. It had always seemed a little short to wear when she went out with Michael; he wouldn't have said anything, of course, far too much the gentleman, but she'd never risked it. But now a sudden surge of recklessness overwhelmed her. If she was going to have lunch with someone as unsuitable as Gil Blake, then she would wear an unsuitable dress. It seemed the perfect choice.

There was no time to wallow in a bath, just enough for a brief shower, then a careful hand with more make-up than she normally wore. She mustn't overdo it. She twisted her hair into a loose knot, leaving tendrils to curl around her cheeks, and then sprayed her neck with a scent she normally kept for the evening. She screwed large gypsy loops into her ears and smiled at the result in the mirror.

She stepped into the black figure-hugging dress which showed every curve to perfection and displayed rather more sheer black nylon-clad leg than she felt quite comfortable with, but it was too late to change her mind. She adjusted the soft cowl neck, until she was satisfied, and then stepped into high-heeled black shoes. Grabbing a black cashmere serape, Casey picked up her tiny bag and, with a final glance in the mirror, opened the door and descended the stairs. It was five minutes to one. It would take her ten minutes to get to the Bell. Just about right. Long enough to keep him waiting. Not so long that he would leave.

She followed two businessmen into the Bell and he didn't see her immediately. He was staring into the fire, his foot propped on the fender. His hair wasn't as wild or as long as it had been, but it was still thick and black and curled boyishly on to his forehead. His nose still had the endearing kink where it had once been broken. He wasn't wearing the jeans or denim jacket that he had lived in; he wouldn't be allowed into the Bell's dining-room if he were. But the expensive and elegant cut of his suit took her by surprise. Not that it disguised his broad figure, and the snowy collar of his shirt only emphasised the strong tanned column of his neck. He glanced up then and she saw the start of surprise, a frown quickly hidden, as he rose to greet her.

'Casey, you're late. Come and sit down by the fire.' His eyes, as he took her hands, lingered momentarily on the black dress, then he looked into her eyes with the smallest smile. 'You must be chilly.' Casey blushed, regretting the stupid impulse that had driven her to such an exclusive inn in a dress that could raise Gil Blake's eyebrows. 'I ordered champagne. It seemed appropriate.' He leaned forward and lifted the bottle from the silver ice-bucket and poured two glasses. He picked them up and gave one to her. 'To old times?'

She raised her glass uncertainly and sipped.

'As you were late I ordered for you. I hope you don't mind?'

This assured, elegant man was a stranger. He wasn't the wild young man who had stolen her heart, and very nearly everything else, all those years ago. 'Gil!' Her urgent whisper was a plea and he raised a practised brow.

'Is something wrong?' he asked, glancing down at his suit. 'Were you expecting overalls and a T-shirt?' He indicated her own appearance. 'If so, my dear, you're a little over . . . no, let's not exaggerate. Nobody could call you over-dressed.'

'If I had known that you invited me here to be insulting, I wouldn't have come,' she hissed angrily.

'I invited you to have lunch with me in order to discuss a business proposition. If I had realised you were going to arrive dressed like an expensive whore I would have taken you somewhere else.' His smile did not quite reach his eyes.

Red patches darkened her cheekbones. 'I bow to your experience in these matters, Gil. Personally I have never met a whore, expensive or otherwise.'

'Your table is ready now, sir. If you would like to follow me.' The arrival of the waiter stopped the angry exchange. Gil rose and stood aside for her to follow the waiter. At the doorway to the restaurant Casey paused, very sorry that she had not worn the conservative grey suit. She took a deep breath and launched herself across the restaurant, aware that every man's eye was upon her. She took her time, indeed she had little choice in the high heels and close-fitting skirt, and at least had the heady satisfaction of seeing cold anger in Gil Blake's eyes as he took his place opposite her at the table.

'Quite a performance, Casey. Please don't repeat it.'

'You can be sure that I won't. I have no plans to repeat this experience. Ever.'

Her fierceness brought a faint smile to his lips. 'I have a proposition for you. Wait until you've heard it before you make any rash predictions.'

She waited. He began to eat the avocado mousse. 'Well?' she demanded.

He was amused and indicated her plate. 'Pleasure before business, sweetheart. I want you to enjoy your food.' The wine waiter produced a bottle and

Gil indicated that he should open it.

Casey seethed inwardly, but she was not about to make a scene in a restaurant where she was well known, and she was sure Gil knew that too. It had been a mistake to come. She should have listened to her first instinct and stayed at home, sorting Brownie jumble. And when she did get home this dress would be on top of the pile. The only way to retrieve her dignity was to eat her lunch and then say goodbye to this Gil Blake. She didn't know him. And she didn't want to.

The mousse was followed by a rare fillet steak with tiny spring vegetables. Casey barely tasted it and refused a dessert, or brandy.

'I'll just have coffee, please. I'm driving.'

'Is that why you didn't drink your wine? I thought perhaps I'd picked something you didn't like.'

'Your taste is excellent. I am sure you don't need me to tell you that. You had something to say to me, I believe?'

Casey pointedly looked at her watch.

'No hurry.' Elbows propped on the table, he slowly unwrapped a chocolate mint between long fingers that hadn't laid a brick in a very long time. 'I thought you would want to know what I've been doing since the last time we met.'

'I'm not in the least bit interested,' she lied.

He smiled, it seemed with genuine amusement, and she had the grace to blush. 'It doesn't matter. I'm going to tell you anyway. Sure about the brandy? I could always have you driven home.' She nodded tightly. 'Very well. Now when you had me sacked . . . ' Casey opened her mouth to protest but Gil shook his finger at her. 'Wait until I've finished. When you had me sacked because I didn't know when to draw the line with the boss's daughter, I went to Australia. It seemed necessary, you understand, to put that sort of distance between us.'

'No!' It hadn't been like that. She

had threatened, but her anger had been at herself, not him. She had never told her father. And, when she had gone looking for him, Gil had gone. Just gone.

There was a muscle working near his mouth, his eyes were slate as he continued. 'I asked you not to interrupt. But I'll grant you the fact that you didn't know you were playing with fire. And I should have realised you weren't like any other girl I'd ever been out with. You were a sheltered little flower, weren't you?' His eyes dropped to the dress. 'That, at least, seems to have changed.'

She wanted to stand up and shout at him that it hadn't, she was just the same, except that she was older, and had hoped wiser. But she sat and listened to him tell her the story of how he had worked for a wage during the week and built first one house at the weekends, then two, and then had launched himself in his own company.

'Have you come back to settle?' she asked, finally.

45

'Oh, yes.' The words were almost a threat and the smile that accompanied them was no different. 'I've sold Blake Estates and I've come home.'

'Home?'

'Yes. I'm buying a business here in Melchester and I'm getting married.'

It took a moment for the words to sink in and the sudden cold spot in the pit of her stomach was an unwelcome reminder of how much she had wanted him and that he was as attractive and dangerous as he had always been. 'You're getting married?'

'Yes, as soon as the contracts are signed.'

'Contracts? You've lost me, Gil.'

'I've no doubt that I did that a long time ago. I could hardly expect you to remain . . . untouched. You live away from home; you've been Michael Hetherington's faithful companion for a long time. It wouldn't be realistic. And I am a realist.' His dark eyes held no hint of humour as he fixed and held her with a look that pinned her to her seat.

'How do you know . . . ?'

'I just know. I made it my business to know. I've kept a close watch on the O'Connor family. I even know that Michael Hetherington is pressing you for a date for the wedding.'

'How on earth . . . ?'

'Why aren't you wearing an engagement ring?' He cut her off in mid-sentence.

'That's none of your business!'

'I intend to make it my business. Right now.' His grey eyes were chilling in his still face. 'This is my proposition. I'll save your father from bankruptcy. In return I want O'Connor Construction. And I want you.'

She laughed nervously. 'That's silly.' His face was expressionless. 'My father's not going bankrupt.' He said nothing. 'Gil?' He meant it. With deepening apprehension she realised that he really meant it. And Casey thought about how distracted her father had been, and how few houses had been sold on the new estates. 'I think I might have that brandy after all,' she said faintly, and it seemed but seconds before it was in her hands and she was sipping the fiery liquid.

'I don't want you to be under any illusion about the situation. Your father has nowhere left to turn. Only you have the power to save him. If he thinks you're marrying me because you want to, it will make it easier for him. But that's between the two of you. You may not wish to make it easy for him. He's been a fool.' He glanced out of the window towards the river.

'But, as you've already pointed out, I'm marrying Michael,' she said desperately.

His eyes came back to hers and his smile froze her. 'Which one is he? Hetherington, Hetherington or Hetherington?'

'None of them,' she snapped.

'Not even a partner? Do you think he will be able to bail out your father? He'll have to dig deep. Your father is in

48

a lot of trouble.' His face was quite without expression. 'Perhaps he'll think you're worth it. He has the advantage of me.'

Casey had listened with a rising tide of panic. Gil Blake knew altogether too much about what had been happening. 'How do you know? That Dad's in trouble.'

'Because I made it my business to know. He always sailed a bit close to the wind and mostly got away with it. Sooner or later he was bound to come unstuck . . . his sort always do. All I had to do was wait.'

He smiled and sat back, satisfied that he had at last made his point, and finally consumed the mint chocolate.

Casey stared at the stranger across the table. 'Why marriage, Gil?' she asked at last. 'Surely your purpose would be adequately served without the blessing of the church?'

Gil's smile disappeared. 'So that you could go running back to Hetherington after the nasty man had finished with you? No, Casey. All or nothing.' She stood up then, unable to sit and listen to this nightmare. She could almost hear the sound of her heart breaking.

Gil Blake rose and handed her a card. 'You and I, Casey, have unfinished business. Call that number when you've made your decision. All you have to say is 'Yes' or 'No'.'

She faced him, white-faced, across the table. 'I'll tell you now, Gil Blake. The answer is no.'

'I'll be waiting to hear from you. Don't take too long. I might change my mind.' He nodded as if satisfied he had made his point. 'You can go now.'

She opened her mouth. Then closed it again. She had been dismissed. Casey turned on her stiletto heels and retraced her steps across the restaurant, this time without the doubtful pleasure of embarrassing Gil Blake. The *maître d'* handed her the serape and, head as high as it would go, she left the Bell, vowing inwardly never to step inside its doors again.

* * *

It was barely light when she woke. Casey opened her eyes and for a fleeting moment of panic struggled against the weight pressing against her. Then Gil stirred and her whereabouts became blindingly clear. She was pressed firmly against the chest of the man she had married, his naked body curled along the length of her back, and they were lying together like spoons in the sagging middle of the old mattress.

He must have slipped in beside her in the small hours, and now lay against her, his deep, even breathing declaring him to be fast asleep.

Casey lay rigid for a moment, then, when he made no further move, she relaxed, allowing herself the luxury of his body against hers, enjoying the warm masculine smell of him, remembering how much she had wanted just this. How easy it would be to turn in his arms, wake him with a kiss, let him make love to her.

Too easy. He had chosen to humiliate her and she hardened her heart. She let out a slow breath and eased herself out of the bed. The wardrobe door creaked as she opened it. He stirred and rolled on to his back, his arm flung out across the space she had so recently vacated.

In sleep he looked younger; a dark wayward curl had fallen over his forehead. He was almost the Gil Blake she had known six years before and fallen head over heels in love with. Almost. She quickly grabbed a handful of clothes and beat a hasty retreat to the safety of the downstairs loo with its washbasin and mirror and lock on the door. Washed, dressed, her hair plaited, she felt more in control of herself. While the kettle boiled she had a closer look at the contents of the cupboards. There wasn't much, but there was some washing powder.

She was standing on the little table unhooking the nets when she heard Gil on the stairs.

'I'm glad to see you're at least taking

your domestic duties seriously,' he said, walking over to her as she unhooked the final loop. He put up his hands and placed them around her waist. His mouth curved into a mocking smile as she started at his touch. 'Jump down, there's a good girl. I could do with some breakfast.' Her arms full of nets, she could do nothing but allow him to swing her lightly to the floor.

'Perhaps you would be kind enough to fetch the nets from upstairs while I get on with it,' she suggested, putting as much chill into her voice as she knew how.

'No, thanks. I'm off to get a paper. It'll give you something to do while I'm at work.'

'Work! But . . . it's Sunday!'

He raised one questioning brow. 'Perhaps you'd like to suggest some more entertaining way to spend the morning?' A flush darkened her cheeks and she stepped sharply back. 'No. I thought not.' He turned as he opened the front door. 'You've got a cobweb in your hair.'

She angrily brushed it away, dumped the nets and stormed into the scullery. The fridge yielded some bacon and half a dozen eggs and very little else.

Gil ate, giving his full attention to the newspaper, leaving Casey to fume in silence. Finally he pushed his chair back and stood up. 'I'll be back for lunch,' he said.

'Not here, you won't! There's no food!'

'Just as well I booked a table at the the Watermill, then, isn't it? They do a very good roast beef.'

'Oh,' Casey said, the wind taken from her sails. 'What time have you booked for?'

'The late sitting at two o'clock. I anticipated that we might be rather occupied this morning,' Gil replied.

'Then you were right! I shall certainly be very busy. It will take me all morning to make any impression on this room.'

'That's the idea. Keep busy.' He

showed his teeth in the semblance of a smile. 'I noticed that the windows could do with a good clean if you've got time.'

'I haven't got a ladder,' she shot back at him.

'No ladder?' he mocked. 'But that's terrible. Have you looked in the shed?' He shook his head sadly. 'Whatever sort of husband deprives his wife of such simple necessities?'

'An unwanted one,' she said coldly, and gasped as his hand gripped her arm, his fingers biting into the soft flesh.

'No, Casey. You made your choice. You walked up the aisle of the church on your own two feet and promised to love and cherish me . . . for as long as you live. I intend to keep you to that.' He released her and she staggered back from him. 'Now I suggest you make a start or you won't be finished by lunchtime.'

Cold fury carried her through the first assault on the dirt. It was all so different from what she had planned.

As she rinsed the dirt from the net curtains she allowed her mind to drift to the designs that she had taken such care over for the house she should have come to as a bride. The large drawingroom looking out across the hills, the cherry-wood kitchen, the warm, comfortable bathroom.

Through the kitchen window she caught sight of a small black and white cat watching her intently from the wall and she smiled at it. The cat jumped down and when she went outside to hang out the nets it brushed up against her legs, mewing pathetically.

'Hello, Mog.' She bent down and rubbed its head. 'What's your name?' The cat purred and she was glad of its company when she gingerly explored the dark, spidery shed for a stepladder. She gave it a saucer of milk and set about the windows.

As she polished the glass and regarded the grey terrace of houses opposite she sighed. There was no point in dwelling on what might have been.

Annisgarth was gone. Her father had sold it to pay the bank and she would have to make the best of what she had. If Gil had loved her it wouldn't have mattered what the house was like. She would have lived with him in a cave.

But he didn't. She was part of the package of revenge. Her father had sacked him and he blamed her. And he had paid them both back. He had bought them body and soul.

By one o'clock she had finished. The little room shone. Satisfied, she turned her attention to her own appearance.

She had brushed her hair, twisted it up into a soft knot and anchored it with tortoiseshell pins and was regarding the contents of her wardrobe when she heard Gil's key in the latch. Hurriedly she snatched a turquoise jersey shirt dress with a matching suede belt and scrambled into it as he ran up the stairs. He regarded her with interest as, hands not quite steady, she fastened pearl studs to her ears.

'Very pretty.'

She looked down at her dress. 'Thank you.'

'I wasn't referring to the dress.' He checked his watch, seemingly unconscious of her heightened colour. 'We'd better get going.'

The Watermill was full, but Gil caught the head waiter's eye and was shown to a table by the window, overlooking the weir. A bottle of champagne was immediately produced and the wine waiter opened it with great ceremony, attracting the attention and smiles of other diners. Gil raised a glass.

'To us, Casey.' If his smile seemed a little grim only she was aware of it. ' "Till death us do part".'

'That sounds less like a toast than a life sentence,' she murmured.

'As you like, sweetheart. But it's a two-way sentence. We're both captives.'

A dull ache in her throat threatened quite suddenly to overwhelm her and she made a hurried dash for the powder-room. She locked herself in a cubicle and stuffed her knuckles into her mouth to stop herself from screaming out loud. Gradually she regained some semblance of control, but as she raised her hand to unlock the door she heard voices.

'Did you see Casey O'Connor with that man she's married?'

Casey felt the colour drain from her face.

'I can certainly see the attraction. Makes Michael Hetherington look a bit weedy.'

There was the sound of water running. 'It was all rather sudden, wasn't it? Do you think she's pregnant?'

'What? The ice maiden?' The woman laughed derisively. 'No, the talk at the Club is that it was his money she was after. He's rich as Croesus, apparently.'

'God, some women don't know they're born, do they?' Their voices trailed away and Casey released the lock. She had to go back into the dining-room and pretend she had never heard that conversation. She caught sight of herself in the mirror, her eyes huge in her pale face, and smiled wanly at herself. Every inch a day-old bride. She smoothed her skirt, lifted her head and prepared to face the world.

As soon as she left the ladies' room she saw the two women who had been talking about her. They exchanged a glance, clearly wondering if they had been overheard. Casey knew them by sight and greeted them politely in passing, not betraying by one twitch her urgent desire to scratch their eyes out, and she smiled brilliantly at Gil as he stood up at her approach.

'Are you all right?' he asked, clearly disconcerted by the warmth of her smile.

'Wonderful,' she affirmed, raising her glass, giving a sparkling imitation of a happy newlywed for the benefit of anyone in the room who had any doubts on that score.

His brows contracted in a frown and

he leaned across the table. 'What's the matter?'

'Nothing,' she said gaily, but her eyes were overbright and he wasn't fooled.

The waiter appeared to take their order and Gil had to leave it, but as soon as the man had gone he resumed his inquisition.

'Tell me what has happened.' As she opened her mouth to deny that anything had, he stopped her. 'Don't say 'nothing'. Clearly something has upset you.'

Casey looked at him in disbelief. 'Upset me?' she whispered.

He shook his head impatiently. 'Something else,' he pressed.

She capitulated. 'I suffered the fate of all eavesdroppers, Gil. I heard nothing good about myself.'

'Oh?' he said dangerously.

'It seems that opinion is divided on my reason for marrying you in such haste.'

'Oh!' He visibly relaxed and his mouth curved in a grin. 'I think I can guess the more obvious reason. What was the alternative?'

'Your money. You are thought to be as 'rich as Croesus'.'

His crack of laughter drew amused glances. 'You could tell them different, couldn't you, my love? On both counts.'

Casey felt herself colouring. 'For goodness' sake, Gil!' she hissed.

'It's not very flattering, you know. I have other ... attributes that any female might find desirable in a husband. Give me your hand.'

He propped his elbow on the table and extended his hand towards her. 'What ... ?'

'Your hand, Mrs Blake.'

Unwilling to make a scene, she laid the tips of her fingers on his, and without warning he bent his head and kissed them. 'Gil!'

He lifted his eyes, unfathomable in the dark tanned face. 'I thought we might play a game, Casey. Perhaps we can convince these gossipers that we married for plain simple lust. That would really give them something to talk about.'

Casey, her hand still captive in his, shook her head. 'No. You didn't let me finish telling you what I overheard. Pregnancy, it seems, was ruled out. The 'ice maiden' doesn't go in for lust.' She withdrew her hand as the waiter appeared with their potted shrimps.

Gil hesitated before he picked up his fork, a strange glint lighting the depths of his grey eyes. 'Ice maiden?' he queried. 'Perhaps they were better informed than I had supposed,' he said finally.

'Undoubtedly. I did, after all, marry you for your money.'

'I'm sorry I'm such a disappointment.'

When they returned home, Gil opened the car door and saw Casey inside the house. 'I have to go back to the office for a while, Casey. I need to make some calls. There isn't a phone here.'

Torn between regret and relief, Casey

watched him drive away. She changed back into jeans and a sweatshirt and began to unpack some of her possessions. Her Chinese lamp and some china figures made the living-room seem a little more like home, and she unpacked her own good cooking utensils and put them away on the kitchen shelves.

She spent the rest of the evening measuring rooms and windows, trailed nosily around by the cat, who settled by her feet while she prepared basic room layouts. She would begin organising the alterations to the house as soon as she got to her drawing-board at the office, in the morning. And the first priority would be a bathroom.

She made herself a sandwich and worked on until she was stiff and cold. She had tried to ignore Gil's long absence, but by ten o'clock cold anger drove her to bed. She left a note propped on the mantelpiece — 'Your supper is in the cupboard' — and lay rigid and sleepless in the white silk pyjamas that Charlotte had thought appropriately sexy honeymoon night-wear.

As she lay there she heard the car draw up outside and the key in the lock. She closed her eyes and pretended sleep as she heard Gil's feet on the stairs. If she thought he wouldn't disturb her, she was mistaken.

He dropped the note on her pillow and yanked back the bedclothes. 'Not funny, Casey. Scrambled eggs on toast will do very nicely.'

Casey opened her eyes slowly. 'It's late.'

'In that case you'd better get on with it and then you can get to sleep.' His eyes travelled the length of her body, barely concealed under the clinging silk. 'I think you'd better move now, Casey. Before I forget that I'm a gentleman,' he said softly.

She swallowed hard and swung her feet to the floor, feeling altogether safer inside the flimsy matching wrap. 'Scrambled eggs?'

He caught her arm. 'Why don't you have some with me?'

'Well, thank you, kind sir,' she flashed at him and pulled free. She sketched a curtsy and then fled as his face darkened and he made a move towards her.

She took her temper out on the eggs and lit the gas, promising herself that she would collect their wedding presents from her parents' home next day. At least they had gone away and she wouldn't have to face her mother's delicate probing. They should already be aboard ship and setting off on a month-long cruise. A second honeymoon. 'Ha!' she said loudly, banging the saucepan down on the gas and lighting the grill for the toast. 'A second honeymoon. A first honeymoon would be something,' she muttered.

'Find everything?' She looked up to find Gil watching her with undisguised amusement.

'No!' she retorted, flushing angrily. 'I shall want the car tomorrow to collect the microwave, and the toaster and the electric kettle . . . '

'Do you think the wiring will stand all that modern technology?' he enquired.

'It will by the time I've finished with it!' she said, stirring the eggs.

'You're planning to modernise this old place?' he asked, surprised.

She buttered the toast and spooned on the eggs. 'Of course. You may have brought me to an antiquated dump, Gil Blake, but it doesn't have to stay that way.' She handed him the eggs. 'Now, if you don't mind, I'm going to bed.' She pulled her wrap around her and waited for him to move aside to let her by.

'I hadn't thought that you would modernise the place,' he said, and for a moment Casey thought he looked slightly nonplussed. Then with a slight smile he stepped aside. 'I'll see you later. Thanks for the supper.'

'If you expect me to say 'any time', forget it!'

She was still awake when he came to bed. Casey clung stiffly to her side of the bed, fighting the treacherous sag in the mattress that tried to drag her to the centre. Ignoring the light, he undressed quickly in the dark and slipped in beside her. For a moment they lay there, together but apart, then Gil murmured, 'Goodnight, Casey,' turned over, and in minutes was breathing in the slow even tempo of sleep.

3

Casey woke to the sound of a cup being placed on the table beside the bed. Her eyes flew open in surprise. Charlotte rarely made it to the kitchen before her.

'Charlie . . . ?' Gil's face was pale above her.

'Who is Charlie?' he asked, a dangerous stillness about him that Casey absorbed with interest.

'Charlie's . . . ' She paused, and a tiny devil prompted her. 'Charlie's just a friend.'

A muscle worked at the corner of his mouth. 'A friend who brings you early morning tea?'

She smiled sweetly. 'Not very often,' she replied with some truth. Gil was already dressed in a navy pin-striped suit, with a snowy shirt and a dark tie with a small crest. He tore his eyes from hers and glanced at the wafer-thin gold watch on his wrist.

'You can tell me all about him later. I have an early appointment.'

Casey swung out of bed. 'I'll come with you. I need the car.'

'I'm sorry, Casey. Not today. I'll arrange for the wedding gifts to be picked up and brought around this afternoon if you like.'

'But . . . '

A wry smile crinkled his eyes. 'If you were considering the use of your parents' bathroom I'm afraid I have to disappoint you.' He turned to go. 'You'll just have to get used to the tin job.'

She took a step after him. 'I haven't noticed that you've been in any hurry to use it,' she threw at him.

'Tonight, dear wife. I promise you that tonight you shall have the pleasure of washing my back in front of the fire.' He smiled. 'And if you're very good I'll perform the same service for you.' He produced some notes from his wallet and placed them on the table. 'House-keeping. Don't spend it all at once.'

Casey ignored the money. 'I spend that much at the hairdresser's,' she threw at him with total disregard for the truth.

His gaze rested on her tousled head for a moment. 'You've been robbed. And if you want to eat I would suggest you learn to do your hair yourself.'

She was left speechless as he ran lightly down the stairs and out of the house.

'Damn him!' She dressed and regarded the pile of washing accumulating in the laundry basket with distaste. With a sinking feeling she acknowledged that she would have to tackle the ancient twin tub in the back scullery very soon.

An hour later she stood at the bus-stop waiting for a bus to take her into town. She had no idea of the fare and it took a moment to register that the driver was refusing to take her proffered note.

'You have to give the correct fare,' the woman in the front seat informed her sternly, and she was conscious of the

71

grumbling behind her as she fumbled for change. She settled herself finally in a seat near the back upstairs only to discover that was where all the smokers went. Rather then draw further attention to herself she suffered.

The bus dropped her on the outskirts of Melchester and she began the long walk up the hill to the flat she had shared with Charlotte. Gil Blake might think he was clever, but he was not denying her the use of a civilised bathroom. Charlotte would be at work and in any case wouldn't mind. Not that Casey had any intention that she should find out. If anyone saw her she would merely be collecting her post.

She ran up the stairs, opened her bag and took out the large keyring that contained all but her car keys. She sorted through them and then, puzzled, went through them again. A third examination confirmed what she had been unwilling to believe. The flat key was missing. And there was no doubt in her mind why it was missing. Gil was absolutely determined that she should not be able to escape his horrible tin bath. Well, she would show him.

She swept back down into the town centre on a tide of indignation. She hardly noticed the distance and it was no time at all before she was standing before the reception desk of the Melchester Hotel.

'Can I help you, madam?' Casey saw the assessing look that the receptionist gave her. A glance in the mirror behind him confirmed that her somewhat dishevelled appearance after her pre-cipitate charge into the town centre was out of place in these elegant surround-ings.

'I should like a room, please. With a bathroom.'

'Twin or double bed?'

'It doesn't matter.'

The receptionist peered over the counter. 'How long will you be staying, madam?' he asked.

'An hour should about do it,' she said without thinking. The man's eyebrows shot up and Casey realised she had made a mistake. 'My bathroom is being refitted,' she said, crossing her fingers. 'I just want a bath.'

'I see. Perhaps, then, I could ask you to pay in advance,' he said primly.

'Of course,' she said, beyond caring what the man was thinking.

He pushed a card across the counter. 'If you could just fill that in for me.' He handed her a pen. As Casey looked up to take it from him, the reflection in the mirror behind the receptionist held her riveted to the spot. But this time it was not her own appearance that was the object of her scrutiny.

Scarcely able to believe what she was seeing, she swung round just in time to see Gil, his arm around a curvaceous brunette, stepping into the lift. He never saw her; his eyes were only for the dark-haired beauty smiling up into his eyes.

'It's been hell without you, darling,' his voice carried to her. 'I don't know how I've managed.' The woman laughed and murmured something that Casey could not hear. Then Gil pressed the button and the lift doors slid together.

Casey dropped the pen as if it burned her fingers, fled from the hotel, and, crossing the road, oblivious to the traffic, sank on to a bench in the little square of park opposite.

She knew she ought to cry. It would help. Her eyes and throat ached with the need for tears, but it hurt too much to cry. Instead she sat, totally oblivious as shoppers sat beside her to rest for a while and toddlers played around her. She tried to analyse the pain that had stabbed through her when she had seen Gil with the woman he called 'darling'. There was only one word to describe it. Jealousy. Dark green jealousy.

'Casey?' She jumped as the man spoke to her, and it was a minute before she realised who he was. Then the round, slightly comical figure swam into focus.

'Philip? I'm sorry, I didn't see you.

How are you?' she asked with automatic politeness.

'I'm fine.' He looked at her oddly. 'But you don't look so hot. You've been sitting here rather a long time. Why don't you come and have a cup of coffee?' Without waiting for her answer he took her arm and led her across the road and into the treasure trove of his shop, Casey's favourite place to choose fabrics and accessories for her interiors.

'I'm glad to see you, actually, old thing. I've been wondering how on earth to get hold of you.'

'Well, you could just have phoned . . .' No, of course he couldn't.

'I've had the offer of a commission for you. From a London architect, no less. Your fame is spreading. Lovely old place. Just up your street.'

She frowned. 'Why did they come to you?'

'I've worked for them before . . .' he grinned wickedly ' . . . but I had to tell them that you would be out of play for a week or two in some sundrenched love-nest. And even then I wasn't sure if you'd be working again.'

'Yes.' The word jerked from her. 'Yes, Philip,' she repeated more gently. 'I'm looking for work.' Tears suddenly threatened, and he whisked her off on a conducted tour of his new stock, regaling her at the same time with scandalous titbits about past clients until he was sure that she was back in control.

After a while what he was saying began to sink in and she started to take some notice of the things he showed her. 'This is lovely. It's just the sort of fabric I need to cover a couple of armchairs. Have you got anything that will match it for curtains?'

'Over here. I can let you have it at a good price,' he said, waggling his eyebrows comically. 'If you spend some of your new client's money in here.'

She laughed. 'Of course, Philip. You don't have to bribe me. Where else would I go? Tell me about this job.'

'You were serious about needing the work, then?'

'I have just moved into an old artisan's cottage. I should think the last time it was done over was for the Coronation. It needs everything.' Including a bathroom, but she wasn't about to hand him that juicy item of gossip.

'But I thought . . . ?' He stopped at the discouragement in her face and changed the subject. 'You're not going to have a lot of time to spend on running up loose covers if you take on this house. They want it yesterday.' He grinned. 'Tell you what, I'll have them made up for you as a wedding present. And the curtains too.'

She tried to thank him. Instead tears began to pour down her cheeks. Philip tutted, gave her his handkerchief and rushed off to make some fresh coffee.

It was as well, she decided, that she had got the tears out of the way before he showed her the valuable commission being offered her. When he spread the plans in front of her she felt a cold chill seize her and for a moment was unable to say anything. It was Annisgarth.

After that appalling lunch with Gil, when he had told her that her father was in deep trouble, she had gone to the office and taxed him with it, hoping, expecting him to deny it. But there had almost been a sigh of relief as he unburdened himself to her.

'I don't know how your friend knows I'm in trouble, but there's no point in beating about the bush, Casey. It was the land below Hillside. I'm going to have to pile it.' He opened the drinks cabinet and poured himself a large Scotch and it occurred to her that it was not his first. 'To put it bluntly, I've been all kinds of a fool. I knew there was competition for that parcel of land and I took a chance and clinched the deal before the test bore results came back. I'd have lost it if I hadn't.' He took a long pull on his drink. 'And 'Lucky' Jim never loses. I'm a victim of my own myth.' He stared out of the window, down into the elegant Georgian square that housed his office. 'House prices were going through the roof; it seemed impossible to pay too much.' She put out a comforting hand. 'I was wrong. And now the foundations are going to cost me an extra ten grand a plot.' He lifted his head and tossed the whisky back. 'Then interest rates started to rocket.' He turned to look at his daughter. 'I can't afford to build, Casey, and I can't sell the land at any price.'

'But surely there are other assets. The company is land rich. There's the new estate.'

'I delayed it too long, Casey. I saw the market rising and I thought I could just get a bit more for the houses if I waited. I was greedy. It finishes us all in the end.'

Casey's world was crumbling about her. 'Does Mother know?' she asked.

'Not yet. I've been trying to tell her for a week.' He turned, his face white. 'You see, I borrowed against the house. I've done it a dozen times, I didn't think Lucky Jim could ever come unstuck . . . Dear heaven, Casey, it's going to break her heart. She deserves better.' He rubbed his hand over his face, hoping she wouldn't notice the wetness he wiped away. 'I've let her down.'

'No!' She stood up and paced the floor. 'There must be something we can do.' She came to a halt and turned to face him. 'My house? Have you borrowed on that?'

James O'Connor looked shocked, misunderstanding her meaning. 'Don't be silly, Casey. That's in your name. I couldn't touch it.'

'Then that's the answer. Sell it.'

'But Casey — '

'Sell it, Dad.'

A ray of hope lit her father's eyes. 'There is someone. A man who's been trying to buy it from me for two or three years. Even when I had tenants in he wanted it. He'd give me a good price too.' Then the light died and he shook his head. 'I can't do this to you. And what about Michael?'

'Dad, sell the house. Don't even think about it.' She hesitated. Perhaps now was a good a moment to tell him. 'I won't be marrying Michael.'

Her father's eyes narrowed. 'Has he got wind of this? If his mother knew . . . '

'No, Dad. Michael wanted me to set a date for the wedding when we had lunch last week at the Bell. He'll make someone a wonderful husband. But not me.' How ironic, she thought. When Michael had insisted on setting a date it had been so clear that she couldn't marry him. She was still, after all this time, blindingly in love with Gil Blake.

She smiled reassuringly at her father, her eyes rather bright. 'So I won't be needing the house after all.'

It seemed very important that she convince him, because the only thing that she cared about at that moment was wiping the look of absolute assurance off the face of Gil Blake. No matter what it took.

But before she left the office she made a trip up the great curving staircase to the drawing office. She opened the plan cabinet drawer marked 'Pending' and slid out the dieline prints detailing the structural alterations, still sharp with the smell of ammonia from the copying machine. She spread them out on the plan table for a last look, touching the little details, the alterations she had spent hours working on. Saying goodbye.

An hour later she was sitting on her rock. The sun, low in the sky, was touching a patch of primroses near her feet and turning them pink.

Pulling herself out of a vanished dream, she stared down at the plans. Then she struck a match and set light to the little funeral pyre of her heart's childhood dream and watched it disappear in the breeze-blown smoke. The fire had burned acrid and fierce for just a few minutes before it was over.

But in the end the sale of the house hadn't been enough to save O'Connor

Construction. Not nearly enough.

Casey stared up at Philip now. 'Where did you get this?'

'The architects sent it. There were some structural alterations to be done.' He indicated the plan but she had no need to look. He grinned triumphantly. 'The thing is, Casey, you'd have a free hand. No interference. Whoever the client is, he's seen your work and likes it. He wants you to do it for him.' He giggled and rubbed his hands and joyously repeated, 'Absolutely no interference!'

Casey caught her lower lip between her teeth. It would be so easy. The designs were all ready and waiting in her desk drawer. Even if she would never live there, it would still be something special to see her ideas come to life, to make Annisgarth what she had dreamed it could be.

She would show Gil that he wasn't the only one who knew what it meant to be in business. Besides, in her present circumstances she could hardly afford to be sentimental. 'What's the fee?' she asked.

'Generous.' He told her the sum and she had to agree.

'I need to get to my office, Philip. But I'll come in here first thing tomorrow and you can look at my designs.'

'Don't you want to see the house first?' he asked in amazement.

She shook her head. 'I know this house. By heart. I'll see you in the morning.'

'Don't forget the measurements for your curtains and loose covers,' he called after her.

She waved absently and forced unwilling feet towards the Georgian square that housed O'Connor Construction. Offices that were now the domain of Gil Blake. But it was lunchtime and with any luck she could be in and out without anyone noticing her. Including her husband. Assuming that he wasn't still otherwise occupied.

The receptionist smiled a welcome. 'Hello, Miss . . . sorry, Mrs Blake.

Here's your post.'

'Thanks, Jane. You could have left it in my office.'

'No. It — ' But Casey was already halfway up the stairs, flipping absently through the pile of envelopes. There was nothing important and she opened the door to her office and turned to throw the mail on her desk. Except that there wasn't room to throw anything on it. It was hidden under heaps of files apparently just unpacked from the cardboard file boxes that covered the floor. Her drawing-board had been folded and pushed against the wall and her plan cabinet had disappeared.

The receptionist panted after her. 'I tried to tell you, Mrs Blake.'

'Tell me?' She turned. 'Yes. Perhaps someone had better explain. What on earth is going on here?'

'Mr Blake's personal assistant is to have this suite of offices now. I mean, you won't be working any more, will you?'

'Personal assistant!'

'Have you any objection?' Gil's voice was cool. He turned to the receptionist. 'Your phone lines are going mad; perhaps you would be kind enough to attend to them.' The girl faded from view and left Gil and Casey to confront one another.

'This is my office, Gil,' Casey said, trying to keep her voice even.

'This *was* your office, Casey. Your father may have let you use some of the most expensive office space in Melchester rent free, but then we both know what happened to him. I, on the other hand, am not a philanthropic society. I am a businessman.'

She flushed with anger. It was true that she paid no rent for her office, but she more than made up for that working in the drawing office when she wasn't busy with interiors. But she denied herself the pleasure of uttering the furious response that sprung immediately into her head. She needed her office and a scene with Gil wasn't the best way to get it.

'I have just been given a valuable commission and I need work space. Now,' she added as calmly as she could.

Grudging approval creased his eyes into a smile. 'You're learning fast, Casey. First rule of business — never let the other guy know what you're thinking.' Then he shrugged. 'I'm afraid I can't help you with space, though. Not unless you're prepared to pay the going rate.' She opened her mouth, then closed it again. 'No? Well, as soon as you have found somewhere suitable let me know and I'll have your office furniture delivered.' His smile broadened into a grin. 'I won't charge you for the service.'

'How generous!' Casey's eyes flashed. 'You're absolutely sure that you can spare it? I'd hate you to part with a twenty-year-old desk that your *personal assistant* might need!'

'None of the items in that office were on the inventory when I took over. I assumed they must be your personal property.' He leaned against the doorway. 'Besides, I'm refurbishing this suite of offices. Mrs Forster is used to rather better facilities.'

'Lucky Mrs Forster! You clearly make a better employer than you do a husband!'

The smile disappeared. White lines were drawn sharply down his cheeks as he took a step towards her. 'Perhaps Mrs Forster is a better personal assistant than you are a wife.'

One of the drawing office staff passed the office and glanced in. 'Hi, Casey! Nice to see you back.' He stopped as if to talk. One look at Gil's face discouraged that intention and he moved quickly on.

Casey was in a quandary. She dearly wanted to tell Gil what he could do with his office, his furniture and just about everything else. But she had to work somewhere, so she kept her tongue between her teeth and changed tactics. She tried a smile. 'Gil, I need somewhere to work right now. It wouldn't be for long.'

He returned her smile with interest, and about as much sincerity. 'Why don't you turn the attic into a studio? There's plenty of room up there.'

'But I . . . '

'Yes?' There was a dangerous glint in his eye.

'Nothing.' She suddenly had the very strong feeling that he already knew what she planned for the attic. Her own private room with her own private bed.

'Good. I'll have your furniture sent round, shall I?'

She bowed slightly. 'Thank you. But not too soon. I don't know how the buses run at this time of day.' If she had hoped to shame him she was disappointed.

'Pick up a timetable at the bus station. I'm sure you'll find it useful.' He glanced at his watch. 'Now if you'll excuse me I have an appointment in five minutes.'

'Gladly,' she spat after his retreating back. He paused mid-stride and then carried on until she heard his office door closing with a highly satisfactory slam.

The receptionist smiled as Casey left. 'All sorted out, is it?'

'Yes, all sorted out,' Casey said, forcing a smile in return. 'Bye.'

She walked back into town and two hours later struggled down Ladysmith Terrace laden with paint, rollers and carrier-bags full of food. She let herself in, vowing that, come hell or high water, she would wrest her Metro from Gil. Not, she thought crossly as she made a longed-for cup of tea, that her Metro would be much good for carrying some of the things she would be needing, both for Annisgarth and for Ladysmith Terrace.

She unpacked the shopping and considered what to prepare for their evening meal. A casserole seemed simplest, since she had no idea what time Gil would be coming home, if he bothered to come home at all. She viciously slashed the skin off an innocent carrot, narrowly missing her thumb, counted to ten, and resumed vegetable peeling in a slightly calmer mood.

Instead of giving herself the undoubted pleasure of imagining the carrot was Gil, she dwelt on the less dangerous subject of transport. She was certainly going to need some for work and perhaps, she thought, a van would be rather more practical than the Metro. Gil could keep her car if she could find something cheap. She'd ask Philip's advice. She had the feeling that Gil would be no help at all.

She was well ahead with painting the attic ceiling when a thump at the door reminded her that she was expecting a delivery. The driver and his mate carried her desk and drawing-board up the narrow stairs, but the plan chest wouldn't go. She emptied the drawers and sent it back to the office.

The light was beginning to go, and her back beginning to go with it, when she heard the front door slam. The pleasant smell of food was wafting up the stairs, reminding her that she had had very little to eat all day.

'Casey?' Gil ran up the stairs and stopped in amazement at the transformation she had already made to the attic. 'Been busy?' he asked.

She plied her roller with care, keeping her eyes firmly on her work. 'Extremely busy. I needn't ask you. You had a busy day, didn't you, Gil?'

His eyes narrowed. 'What is that supposed to mean?'

'Nothing. Why should it mean something? It's true, though, isn't it?' she asked innocently.

'Perfectly true.' He indicated the rolls of plans heaped in a corner. 'Why did you send the plan chest back?'

'I thought your need was greater than mine. Consider it a donation to 'business',' she said, concentrating on a difficult corner. She caught sight of his face. 'Actually it wouldn't go up the stairs, and I didn't think it added much in the way of style to the living-room.'

'Perhaps not. Dinner smells good. I

could eat a horse.'

'Be careful what you say, Gil Blake.'

'Is that a threat?' he asked lightly, advancing towards her.

She straightened up. 'No. A promise.' She had finally finished the second wall and stepped back to examine her work. 'Just let me wash the roller and then we can eat.'

She held the roller at arm's length in front of her, and the look in her eyes suggested that, in deference to his suit, discretion was almost certainly the better part of valour. He raised his arms in mock surrender and retreated before her down the stairs, backing into their bedroom as she passed.

Casey had a quick wash and wrapped a towel around her. She paused abruptly in the bedroom door as she realised that Gil was still there.

'I'll light a fire. It's chilly,' he said, eyeing the towel with interest as he tied the lace of his trainer. 'You've missed a bit,' he said, straightening.

'Missed a bit?'

He reached towards her and touched her throat with the tips of his fingers, trailing them down towards her breasts, his eyes laughing as she backed nervously away. 'A drip of paint,' he murmured, and followed her. She was backed up against the bed and, with nowhere else to go, held herself rigid against his resolute advance.

'I thought you had a fire to light,' she said hoarsely, her heart beating a tattoo, quite unable to move from the magnetic pull of bottomless grey eyes.

'A drip of paint,' he repeated, and bent swiftly to kiss the cleft just above the impeding towel. He raised his head and his eyes smiled into hers. 'Just there.' She opened her mouth to protest, but felt quite unequal to the task, and closed it again. 'Warmer now?' he teased gently. She swallowed hard, only too aware that her cheeks were flaming. 'Good. I'll go and light a fire. Or perhaps I already have?' He didn't wait for her reply and she sat suddenly on the bed, her legs not quite capable of holding her.

Why couldn't she do it? Just let the towel fall to the floor and Gil sweep her into his arms to kiss away the hungering need he awoke in her. She remembered the feel of his body pressed against her and knew that she wanted him to hold her, tell her how much he wanted her.

'Stop it!' she scolded herself and with a shuddering sigh forced herself to recall the scene in the Melchester Hotel. No, by heaven. He had compelled her to marry him and he would plead for his release. Perhaps then she might relent.

The fire was burning steadily in the hearth by the time she went downstairs and Gil was stretched out in front of it. Casey raised an eyebrow.

'Hard day?' she asked with heavy irony as he followed her into the kitchen, only too aware of her own aching muscles.

'Pretty hard,' he agreed. 'Meetings all

morning. A working lunch. The bank manager this afternoon.'

She ladled two vegetable-rich helpings of lamb casserole with extreme care on to two plates, perilously close to throwing it. She had witnessed his working lunch.

'Are you sure you can manage dinner?' she asked with dangerous calm. 'These working lunches can be rather . . . rich.'

'This one wasn't. I had a cup of coffee and a sandwich.'

She gazed at him from under long dark lashes. 'I don't suppose you had time for more.'

'You suppose right,' he said sharply.

For a moment she met his unwavering scrutiny, aware that a flight of butterflies had invaded the region of her abdomen. Then he smiled.

'Tell me about this commission you were so fired up about this afternoon.'

As she told him the bare outlines of the deal with Philip he listened thoughtfully. 'So, you've got that commission, have you? We've been doing the alterations to your plans. They're nearly finished.'

'You did them to my plans?' It had been niggling at the back of her mind all afternoon that something was wrong. Philip had had her plans too. She looked at Gil. 'But I . . . ' Her voice trailed away.

'Yes?' he encouraged.

She shook her head. 'Nothing.'

He shrugged. 'We couldn't find the prints, which was a nuisance, but they were on microfilm. Everything's copied, you must know that.'

'Oh. Of course. I didn't think.'

'No, it's a family failing, apparently. What did you do with them?'

'I . . . I had a little bonfire.'

'A bonfire?' he asked, disbelief etched in every feature. 'What on earth for?'

'It was symbolic. An ending. That was all.' She concentrated very hard on the food before her, refusing to look him in the eye.

Gil laid his fork down on his plate

and sat back, satisfaction written clear across his face. 'It will be tough working on the house you were going to share with Hetherington. Decorating it for someone else to live in.'

4

'If you hadn't acted so rashly it could still have been yours. Not with him, of course. He couldn't have afforded you unless his mother had been prepared to put up the money.' He leaned forward. 'How will you feel, do you think, decorating that house and coming back to this one? Back to me?' he added harshly.

Casey stared, shocked at the bitterness in his voice. Michael had never been to Annisgarth. He had never seen the plans. It was the realisation that Gil was the only man that she had ever wanted to share it with that had finally convinced her that she could never marry Michael.

She looked Gil resolutely in the eye. For some reason he was angry and he was trying to upset her and he was succeeding, but she wasn't about to show it.

'I'm a businesswoman, Gil. And there's no room for sentiment in business, I'm sure you will agree.' Casey stood up and dumped the dishes in the sink, clinging momentarily to the edge, biting down hard to prevent the outflow of feelings that his words had aroused. She was trying to think of it as a purely business venture, but the reality was going to take every ounce of self-control she possessed.

'There's cheese and fruit for dessert,' she managed in a calm voice.

'No pudding?'

'If you like puddings you'll have to fetch the microwave.'

'That doesn't sound very promising,' he said, turning his mouth down.

'Don't turn your nose up at what you haven't tasted, mister,' she said, forcing a lightness she was far from feeling into her voice. 'I'm very nifty with a microwave when it comes to puddings. What's your favourite? *Crème caramel*? Lemon sponge? Or are you a spotted dick man?' She turned, smiling, determined that he shouldn't see how upset she was. He had come up behind her and was standing far too close.

He reached out and touched her cheek. 'If you were any sort of a wife you would know that by now, wouldn't you, Mrs Blake?'

'Don't worry. I'll just ask around. I'm sure I wouldn't have to look very far to find someone who would know.' She turned away from him, fiddling with cups, refusing to give him the satisfaction of seeing the angry tears that squeezed from beneath her lids despite her efforts to stop them. 'I'm afraid it'll have to be instant coffee until we get the filter.'

'Instant will be fine,' he replied. She turned and eyed him narrowly, certain that he was laughing at her.

'Really?' She managed to raise an eyebrow.

He shook his head and apologised. 'I'm sorry I didn't manage to get the wedding presents down to you this afternoon.'

'That's all right. I do know how very busy you were.'

'So you said.' Gil regarded her steadily for a moment, then changed the subject. 'I had an idea today.'

'Only one? You must be slipping.'

He ignored this gibe. 'I thought we might have a house-warming party.'

Casey felt her heart skip a beat. But he looked perfectly serious. 'A house-warming party?' she asked dully.

'What do you think?'

'You really don't want me to tell you what I think, Gil.'

He ignored this. 'Nothing excessive. Just a few friends in for dinner. It's time I started to meet some people.'

Casey stood up, her face quite pale. 'You seem to have done quite well so far,' she said with meaning, but he missed the innuendo, or chose to ignore it.

'I don't want to cut you off from your friends. They're all most welcome here. Any time. Should I join the Club, do you think? Or . . . ' he added

103

dangerously, indicating their surroundings ' . . . perhaps they wouldn't allow anyone who lived somewhere as plebeian as Ladysmith Terrace under their hallowed portals.' She put her hand to her mouth to stifle a somewhat hysterical giggle. 'What's so funny?' he demanded.

'They already have a member who lives in Ladysmith Terrace, Gil. Me.'

His face relaxed into a grin. 'Well, let's allow them in on the joke. Give me a few names and telephone numbers and I'll get them invited.'

Clearly he was determined. 'I'll do it myself,' she said as she started to clear the table.

'How? You've no phone.'

'I . . . ' She hesitated, and felt herself colouring as she made the deliberate decision not to mention her portable telephone safely locked away in her desk upstairs. Just in case it went the same way as her car and her flat key. She hurried on. 'I suppose your personal assistant will organise it all beautifully. Perhaps you'd like to invite her? Or is there anyone else you'd like to bring along?' she challenged.

'No. I don't think so.' He watched as she washed the dishes. When they were finished Gil rose. 'Now. I promised you a treat tonight, didn't I?'

Casey stretched her aching muscles. 'A treat?'

He didn't answer; instead he disappeared through the scullery, reappearing moments later with the tin bath balanced in one hand. He threw her a grin as he walked through the kitchen and into the living-room and placed it carefully in front of the fire. Then he worked steadily with a bucket, filling the bath with hot water from the tap.

'Wouldn't a hose be easier?' Casey asked finally.

'It would drip on the carpet. Have you got any bubble bath?' Casey fetched a bottle and he poured some into the water. 'There. You'll look like a film star,' he said, happily.

'Oh, no!' she said, backing away.

'Absolutely. After all that painting. A bath is just what you need.'

'No . . . '

'Ladies first,' he drawled.

Casey's lips tightened. 'No. Thank you.'

Gil tipped in another bucketful and tested the water. 'Perfect. In you get.'

'I think I've made my feelings quite clear, Gil. You can do what you like, but I . . . ' She shrieked as he picked her up and held her over the water. 'Let go of me!'

'We can do this the hard way, or the easy way, Casey. Make a decision.'

She kicked and struggled. 'Put me down!' she demanded.

'If you're sure?'

Words deserted her as he dumped her fully clothed in the tub. 'How dare you?' she finally spat at him.

'But you told me to put you down.' His eyes twinkled as he protested his innocence.

'I didn't mean in the water,' she yelled, starting to get up, then shrieked as he put out a hand and pushed her firmly back under the water. She struggled furiously as the water stuck her trousers to her, soaking through to her underwear. 'Let me up!' she cried, fighting against him. But the water soaked heavily into the wool of her sweater, dragging her back with its weight. 'How could you?' she panted, her breath coming in short furious gasps.

'Oh, it was easy, sweetheart. Believe me.'

'My sweater will be ruined,' she groaned, and lay back in the water, finally giving up the unequal battle.

'Better take it off, then,' Gil suggested helpfully, and obligingly pulled it over her head, squeezing the water out into the bath while she sat gasping and spluttering. 'Now, Casey. I'm going to get a bowl to put your clothes into. You can get out of them yourself while I'm gone if you like, or I'll undress you when I get back.' His face wore an implacable expression as he regarded her steadily. 'I'll give you the option again — the hard way, or the easy way. You choose.' He stood up and carried the dripping sweater into the kitchen.

A sudden panic overtook her at the thought of his hands undressing her and she scrambled to undo buttons, her fingers fumbling desperately in an effort to be finished before he returned.

She dropped the sopping wet bundle into the bowl and Gil regarded her with approval. 'Very wise,' he said. Then a little regretfully, 'But not so much fun.' She slid further under the bubbles as his eyes lingered, and he laughed. 'Fancy a drink? Gin and tonic?' Casey clenched her teeth, refusing to answer. 'Gin and tonic it is, then.'

He disappeared with her wet clothes and reappeared with a tray. He poured two measures of gin, added ice and lemon and topped them up with tonic. He handed her a glass and, after a moment's hesitation, she took it and sipped slowly as the hot water eased away the hard work of the day.

'This is different,' she murmured, watching the flicker of firelight playing against the walls.

'Do you think you could get used to it?'

Casey flickered a glance in his direction. 'You can get used to anything. If you want to.'

He put his glass down on the hearth and sat behind her in the armchair. 'Now my old grandad always enjoyed a sandwich and a brown ale when he had a bath. I never fancied it myself. Almost bound to cause indigestion, I would have thought . . . and what if you dropped your sandwich in the bath?' The idea conjured up was finally too much and she was unable to restrain a giggle.

She stopped abruptly as his hands began to massage her shoulders, his long fingers gently kneading at the stiffness, soothing out the tension. 'How's that?' he asked softly at her ear. She didn't answer but closed her eyes as his fingers began to stroke her neck.

Gil allowed his fingers to stray down her back, his knuckles pressing lightly against her vertebrae, his fingers sliding down to her waist. She held her breath as he rippled up her ribcage. Then his fingertips brushed against her breast in the gentlest caress. But it was a momentary lapse and he immediately withdrew his hands and stood up.

Except that Casey didn't want him to stop. She wanted him to go on, cup her breasts in his hands, hold them. She made a small disappointed moan and opened her eyes to find herself being regarded with ironic amusement. A slow deep flush warmed her face as she realised how she had betrayed herself.

Gil turned his head to one side. 'Listen! Can you hear it?'

'What?' Casey asked, hearing nothing.

'I think it's the devil's teeth chattering,' Gil said, softly.

'Very funny,' she snapped.

He grinned, holding out a bathrobe for her. Casey eyed it nervously but stood up, realising that he wasn't going to go away. She quickly slipped her arms into the sleeves and Gil wrapped it around her, fastening the belt in a firm knot. For a moment he held on to her, regarding her gravely. Then he lifted her out and set her on the floor.

'My turn.' He reached down, pulled off the sweatshirt and threw it on the chair. He unbuckled his belt and slid down the zip. Casey quickly looked away as he removed the rest of his garments and stepped into the water.

He sank down to his chin, closed his eyes and sighed. 'More hot water, please.'

Casey eyed the bucket. 'If you want more hot water I suggest you get it yourself,' and held her breath as he regarded her quizzically, his eyes just above the foam.

'If you like.' He sat up and began to climb out of the bath.

'Wait!' she said, her face crimson. 'I'll do it.'

He sank back under and smiled approvingly. 'Good girl. You're catching on fast.'

'Is that enough?' she demanded after two buckets.

'Another one.' She brought another bucket of hot water and poured it in.

'Anything else I can do for you,' she asked testily.

'How's your massage technique?'

'Not as practised as yours, I suspect.' But she knelt down and tentatively began to massage his wide shoulders. 'Is that right?' she asked.

'A little harder.'

She dug her fingers in and had the pleasure of hearing his sharp intake of breath. Gradually, however, the feel of his well muscled body beneath her fingers eased her temper. 'How's . . . ?' Her voice dried in her throat. She swallowed. 'How's that?'

'Lower,' he murmured. 'Keep going down my back.' She tried to repeat what he had done to her back and he sighed.

'Is that all right?' she asked, uncertainly.

'Much more than all right,' he said, seizing her hand and guiding it to his hard and throbbing loins. 'Wouldn't you say?' he demanded. She snatched her hand away and leapt to her feet. 'No? Ah, well, in that case I'll have another drink.' Her hands shaking, she refilled his glass and passed it to him. 'No ice?' he asked.

Casey picked up the bowl and regarded the ice cubes gradually melting and floating in their own water. She carried it carefully over to Gil and he held out his glass.

'How many cubes do you want?'

'A couple will do,' he said.

She put two small lumps into his glass. 'Sure?'

He looked at his drink. 'Well, perhaps another one.'

'Don't stint yourself, Gil. Why don't you have the lot?' She tipped the bowl and the icy liquid hit him full in the chest. He erupted, gasping, from the water. Casey's blue eyes glinted in the firelight. 'How's your ardour now, Gil?' she asked.

He caught his breath. 'Cooler, my dear,' he acknowledged. 'Decidedly cooler.'

* * *

The following morning she was up at dawn, dressed and breakfasted by the time Gil emerged. Casey looked up from the kitchen table.

'I've made a list of people to invite for dinner. I've suggested next Tuesday, but you may have other plans. Any day after that will suit me.'

'Good morning, Casey.' He ignored the list and sat down heavily opposite her. There was a haggard look about him that suggested a sleepless night.

She dropped the sheet of paper on the table in front of him and smiled brilliantly. 'Good morning, Gil. Would it be too much to ask you to drop me somewhere near the shopping centre this morning? Just to save bus fares, you understand.'

'Oh, I understand perfectly. Breakfast?'

Casey smiled benevolently. 'Bacon and egg? Perhaps a couple of sausages?'

He glared at her. 'How about orange juice and a slice of toast?'

She complied with every outward sign of obedience and half an hour later he deposited her on the edge of the town centre. 'Will you be late tonight?' she asked.

'About six,' he said, tersely.

'Well, if I'm not back, will you start dinner? There are chicken pieces ready in the fridge — they just need popping in the oven.' She was half out of the car when his hand arrested her. She looked back, startled.

'No, Casey. Make sure you *are* back,' he grated.

'Or what, Gil?' she asked quietly.

'Or you can forget being a working wife. Do I make myself clear?'

'As crystal,' she said, icicles dripping

from her tongue. 'But why don't you write a little contract for me just to be sure? One of those with lots of small print. I'm sure you're really good at that.' Two hectic spots stained her cheekbones. 'In fact, I don't understand why you didn't insist that I sign one of those nasty pre-nuptial jobs with a clause to ensure that I never ask you to wash up . . . '

His fingers bit hard into her arm. 'Pre-marital contracts are a protection in case of divorce, Casey. Don't ever allow yourself the comfort of believing that this marriage is anything but permanent.' There was something so deadly earnest about him that Casey, discomfited, allowed her eyes to drop. 'And since this is a public place, and since in public we will at all times make the effort to appear unexceptional newlyweds, you will kiss me before you go.'

'Here?' she asked, startled.

'Here and now.'

Casey swallowed. There was an

unwavering and compelling arrogance about him that brooked no denial. Slowly she leaned forward until his eyes were so close that she could see the small dark flecks in the grey. He made no move towards her, forcing her to come all the way to him. Her lips brushed his with the lightest touch then she moved back. His grip tightened.

'Try a little harder, sweetheart,' he demanded. She closed her eyes to blot out the cynical expression with which he was regarding her and allowed her lips to kiss him in the manner they yearned to. For a brief shocked second he made no response. Then his mouth moved against hers and, for the time it took her heart to ride a high-speed lift to the basement and back, the world contracted until it was nothing but the warm circle of Gil's arms holding her close.

Finally he raised his head and regarded her from under half-closed lids. 'That was a much better effort, my dear.' He leaned over and pushed the car door open. Casey hesitated for a moment. Then, as he made an impatient move, she stumbled out on to the pavement and watched Gil steer the little red car into the morning traffic without so much as a backward glance.

She took a deep steadying breath before tapping on the back door of Philip's store. If he noticed her distracted appearance he said nothing, but indicated the coffee-pot and settled down over her designs.

'These are lovely, Casey,' he said finally. 'Really lovely.' She started as his voice dragged her back from the memory of Gil's mouth on hers. Philip grinned. 'I'm sure it must be hard to think of anything but that gorgeous new husband of yours, but do try and keep your mind on your work, love.'

'Sorry.' She made an effort to concentrate. 'I need some transport, Philip. Any ideas?'

'Price?'

'Well, that's rather the problem. I was hoping you might lend me your old mini van. You scarcely ever use it now.'

He gave her an odd look. 'You'll have to pay the insurance.'

'I think I can manage that.'

He nodded. 'If you really want it you can have it for the duration of the job. Now, let's go and see how this all fits together.'

She kept the tightest rein on her feelings as they pulled up in front of the house, afraid that, despite her bravado to Gil the night before, she might break down.

Philip went inside, but Casey walked up the hill to her favourite spot. Annisgarth lay still and quiet below her, nestled in its hollow. Coming up here had always felt like coming home.

'Casey's Acre', her father called it, although it was nearer two. It had taken him a long time, and a great deal of money, to buy it for her. His little girl's dream house.

They had walked this one Sunday morning when she was quite small and after lunch she had drawn a picture of it. She had put a swing in the old oak tree, and a cat smiling out of the bedroom window, and her father had admired it. 'Are you going to be an architect, child?'

She hadn't known what an architect was. But she had known what she wanted. 'It's where I'm going to live when I grow up,' she'd said. 'The yellow house on the hill.' And there had been a silent pact struck between them over her mother's head.

But she wasn't a little girl any more. She was a married woman and it was time to put childish dreams behind her. She had dwelt for far too long on the memory of an adolescent crush and a few kisses, but the truth was she hadn't wanted to forget. Michael had been a comfortable enough partner. Too comfortable. If he had been a little more forceful as a lover she might perhaps have forgotten Gil. But it wasn't very likely. Even after six years his image had been too potent.

'Damn you, Gil,' she said fiercely,

startling a robin into releasing a worm he had spent a minute tugging from the turf.

The late April breeze was colder than she had thought. Her cheeks were cold and she put her hands up to warm them and found they were wet with tears she had been unaware of shedding.

'Casey!' Philip's voice recalled her to the present. She took one last look at the breathtaking views across the valley before she made her way back to the house and gave her mind to work.

It took all day to get the orders placed and the work crew put together, and it was gone six o'clock before she parked the elderly van behind the Metro.

Gil was slumped in an armchair in front of the fire, a glass in his hand, the living-room floor covered in cardboard boxes. She exclaimed with delight and then the expression on his face brought her to a halt.

'How did you get home?' he demanded,

his eyes like slits.

Casey raised an eyebrow, suspecting that the glass in his hand was not the first. She lifted her hand and jangled the little bunch of keys. 'Philip loaned me a van.'

He stood up a little unsteadily. 'Really? Another of your admirers? You must run a list by me some time so that I can keep track.'

'With pleasure. When I have a spare hour or two,' she said, suppressing the urge to laugh at his idea of Philip as a rival.

'I thought,' he said dangerously, 'that you were going to work from here.'

'I am. I will,' she said. 'It was just easier to work with Philip today. We had to go up to the house, and the orders for goods were all placed through him. He has accounts, special discounts I couldn't get . . . '

'I notice you didn't mention the lack of a telephone.' A chill rippled down her spine. 'Accounts brought me the bill for your portable telephone today.

They wanted to know if I would be paying for it through the company. What portable phone, Casey?'

Slowly she opened her bag. 'This one?' she asked.

'Have you got more than one?' She shook her head. 'Then that must be it.'

'And will you be wanting this too?' She held it out to him. 'Along with my car and the key to my flat?'

'*Your* flat?' She blushed, disconcerted at the anger in his voice. 'This is where you live! In the house I have provided, and no matter what it lacks you'll lump it!' He leaned towards her. 'I'm not having you popping in anywhere else for a quick bath, or anything else, whenever the fancy takes you.' He turned the telephone over in his hands before handing it back to her. 'You might as well have it. If I take it you'll just get another one to take its place. Won't you?' he demanded.

'If you make me,' she affirmed.

He struggled to his feet. 'That, Casey,' he warned, 'is a game two can play. Just be sure and remember that some games are easier to start than finish.'

Casey, an image of the woman in the lift clearly etched into her memory, didn't need his meaning spelt out. 'I'm not particularly interested in games, Gil. This is one that you started,' she reminded him.

He scowled at her for a moment, his thick, well defined brows drawn together, then he swallowed the contents of his glass. 'Hadn't you better get on with the dinner?' he said.

* * *

Casey left Philip to brief the decorating crew who were to start painting the exterior of Annisgarth, and instead concentrated on her own home for a few days. She completed the attic, softening the pristine whiteness with a rose-coloured stencil around the skirting and the windows to match a remnant of carpet that Philip let her have cheaply, and which covered the floor with inches to spare. She left the windows bare for maximum light and set up her drawing-board in front of it.

That done, she began to clear out the little spare bedroom to prepare it for its conversion to a bathroom. She was stripping off a rather gaudy line in floral wallpaper when Gil arrived home on Friday evening. He stood in the doorway and watched her for a moment.

'Why are you decorating up here? I thought you would have started down-stairs,' he asked.

She paused and looked at him. 'Rush to make it respectable before your little dinner party, you mean?'

He shrugged. 'If you like.'

She pulled a large piece of wallpaper down and dropped it with the rest. 'I can't do it properly in a few days and I'm not bodging it up in an effort to impress. Besides, my most pressing need is for a bathroom, and this is going to be it.'

'Bathroom?' He raised an eyebrow. 'I thought perhaps you were planning to move in here . . . '

'Move in here?' she asked, straightening, and noticing the challenge in his eyes. 'Why should I do that, Gil? I have your promise that you'll leave me to decide when I wish to become your . . . 'wife' . . . '

'You already are that, Casey,' he said roughly, his hands clenched. 'Don't ever forget it.'

' . . . and your assurance that you are a gentleman,' she continued as if he had not interrupted. 'So why should I need a separate bedroom to reinforce that promise?' Her look demanded his acknowledgement.

'You . . . ' He stepped forward, his face a mask, then checked himself. He nodded slowly. 'You're quite right, of course. There's absolutely no need. And if I were to change my mind that door would hardly keep me out,' he added matter-of-factly. He stared out of the window down into the yard below.

'There's a cat on the doorstep,' he said absently.

'She thinks she lives here,' Casey said, letting out a breath she had not been aware she was holding and continued to work. 'She's expecting kittens soon. I've been feeding her.'

'That's a relief. I thought you might have been planning to feed me the tins of cat-food I saw in the cupboard.'

'That's a thought.' She hid a smile. 'If you're not busy, why don't you come and give me a hand with this?' she asked.

For a moment she was certain he was going to refuse, then he shrugged. 'Sure. I'll get changed.'

They worked together for a while in silence and broke the back of the work. 'Thanks, Gil.' Casey stripped off her rubber gloves and looked around. 'It won't take long to finish now.'

'There's the small matter of a bathroom suite,' he reminded her, 'if you're hell-bent on this. I rather thought you were beginning to enjoy our fireside baths together.'

Casey chose to ignore this remark. 'Philip told me about some ex-showroom stock that's going cheap at the bathroom place at the business park. I'm going to have a look tomorrow.'

'Well, bully for Philip.' His eyes narrowed thoughtfully. 'I suppose I'd better come with you.'

'Only if you can spare the time from your office,' she murmured. It was the first time in days that he had come home before nine o'clock.

'Perhaps if there was something more than the cold comfort you offer I'd have something to come home for,' he said coldly. 'What's for dinner?'

'Nothing, yet! I've been working too.' Angrily she grabbed the plastic bag full of rubbish and made for the door. He caught her and held her as she passed, pulling her towards him.

'I could get a Chinese if you like,' he offered.

'Isn't that a bit extravagant? Could we afford it *and* a bathroom suite?'

Casey asked, her heart turning treacherous somersaults at his touch.

'I think we'll manage, provided we have egg and chips tomorrow.' His mouth widened into a smile. 'And I don't remember saying that we could afford a bathroom suite. Only that I might be prepared to look.'

'In that case I'll have number twenty-seven, number thirty-two and number sixty-one.'

'Something of a change for you, is it? Chinese food?' he enquired, letting her go.

'You know how it is, Gil. You try new things, but you always come back to your old favourites.'

'Is that so?' He tossed the car keys lightly in the air, a dangerous little glint in the cool grey eyes. 'I wonder what old favourites you've been trying out lately?'

He didn't wait for her answer but the door was banged shut with rather more force than necessary.

Casey shivered. The house was not

very warm; it was still only the very beginning of May and the early warm weather had gone as quickly as it had come. On a sudden impulse she decided to light the fire she had laid earlier. She held the match to the paper and it caught for a moment and then went out.

'Blast! It must be damp.' She tried again; this time the flames caught and held. She sat back on her heels and pushed a stray strand of hair out of her face, unaware of the streak of soot she brushed across her cheek. The wood started to smoke and burn and the coal fell, threatening to put out the little blaze.

'Drat the thing,' she said. It had been her first attempt at laying a fire herself and clearly she hadn't got it quite right. Desperately she stuck a sheet of newspaper over the opening to cause a draught and the flames roared bright and fierce behind the paper.

The sound of a car door closing outside made her turn and the paper slipped, shooting up the chimney in a bright blaze.

'Casey!' Gil thundered from the other side of the front door. 'Casey! Are you all right?' She leapt to her feet and stepped back, knocking the bucket, which fell with a clang against the hearth. She stared for a moment in dismay at the mess on the hearth-rug, but Gil was hammering furiously on the door and there was no time to clear it up. 'Casey. Dear God, for one awful minute — '

'I just thought I'd light a fire,' she said breathlessly. 'I didn't think it was going to work, but it seems all right now.'

'Light a fire! I should think you have damn well lit a fire. I thought you'd set light to the house. Flames just shot out of the chimney pot, for God's sake!'

'Oh, no,' she said airily. 'That was just a sheet of newspaper. I couldn't get it going . . . ' And then she stopped as he seized her shoulders.

'Gil!' she protested.

'Don't ever . . . ' He breathed deeply. 'Don't ever do that again! Promise me!' he demanded.

'It was cold,' she said, feeling suddenly foolish. 'And the paper was damp.'

'Well, setting fire to the house is a pretty drastic remedy for feeling chilly. Next time, I suggest you put on another jumper.' He gave her a little shake. 'Promise me!'

'I . . . I promise,' she said meekly, and stood very still, intensely aware of a current of tension passing between them. He stared down at her for a long moment, then the coals fell in the grate and the moment was gone. His hands dropped from her shoulders.

'Good. Now while you clear up this mess I'll go and rescue our dinner from the doorstep. Always assuming some dog hasn't run off with it.'

'What dog would be that brave?' she said. But quietly.

5

Casey woke next morning to the sound of the front door banging, and lay for a moment relishing the quiet peace. She had taken care to be up very early after that first morning when Gil had left her to sleep on. But there was no rush to get up today, especially now that Gil had gone out. She turned over and when she woke again it was to find Gil standing over her.

'Good morning, Casey. Sorry to wake you, but breakfast wouldn't wait.'

She struggled to sit up, pulling the covers up to her chest. 'Breakfast?'

He placed a tray on her knees. 'I thought our first week together deserved some sort of recognition. Happy anniversary.' He leaned forward and kissed her lightly on the cheek before sitting on the edge of the bed.

The tray contained orange juice,

coffee, fresh croissants and a single red rose. Casey picked it up and leaned forward to breathe in the scent, her long tawny hair falling about her face. She looked up, her eyes shining like twin sapphires.

'It's lovely, Gil. Thank you.'

'Not as lovely as you are, Casey.'

She couldn't think of a reply to such a direct compliment and after an awkward moment Gil made a move to stand up. 'Don't go, Gil. Help me to eat these.'

'Don't you like them?'

'Love them, but they're so fattening!'

'And that's a real problem?' he teased, but took the portion she offered him.

'Do you want to look at bathrooms this morning?' Gil asked.

'You're really not working?'

'I have to go in for a while. But I could be finished by eleven.'

Casey sat back. 'I have Brownies from ten until eleven-thirty. We could go then.'

'Brownies?' he frowned. 'But you're supposed to be on your honeymoon. Suppose I'd whisked you away to the Bahamas for a month?'

'But you didn't,' she pointed out.

'No, I didn't.' He stood up. 'Just as well in the circumstances. It would have been a terrible waste of money, wouldn't it?' She didn't answer. 'Where shall I pick you up?'

'It's in the hall by the Methodist Chapel.'

He nodded. 'I know it.'

An hour later, dressed in a warm navy tracksuit, her hair restrained in a thick plait, she had the girls screaming with excitement in a wild game of Apple Pear Peach Plum.

'I don't know what I'd do without you, Casey,' Matty James said later as the girls disappeared into a sunny May morning. 'I just can't cope with noisy games the way I used to.'

'It's fun. Do you need a lift?'

'No, thanks. Brian's picking me up.'

'Did someone mention my name?'

Brian James could have made a pair of book-ends with Matty. They were both red-cheeked, grey-haired and ample in proportion. Casey grinned a welcome.

'Hello, Brian. How are you?'

'In the pink, my dear, as always.' He shook his head and pursed his lips. 'At least I would be if you would go back to wearing a proper uniform like Matty.'

'This is my new uniform, and very comfortable it is. Much more practical for games.'

Brian eyed Matty lovingly, noting her rather tight navy pinafore dress, blue shirt and neat little bow at the neck. 'The treat of my week, Matty in uniform.' He winked at his wife as she blushed. 'You should try it on that new husband of yours, Casey. He'll tell you there's nothing like a uniform to turn a man's head. I think it's the navy blue stockings.'

'Brian, you stop that right now,' Matty scolded, 'you're making Casey blush.'

Casey shook her head. It wasn't

Brian that was making her blush, it was Gil standing in the doorway, listening to every word. 'Gil,' she said clearly, before they said any more. 'Come and meet Matty and Brian.' She made the introductions and then left Matty to lock up.

She brushed some dust off her tracksuit trousers. 'You don't mind me like this?' she asked Gil, as he opened the car door.

'Not at all. I've never been particularly attracted to women in uniform.'

'I didn't mean . . . Oh!'

'I'm very partial to stockings, though,' he continued as though she had not interrupted. 'Black ones . . . with long suspenders. Just in case you're interested.'

'Not in the least,' Casey responded hotly.

'I think that's a dreadful pity,' he said, and she was grateful that their arrival at the showroom put a stop to the conversation.

He took no part in choosing the

bathroom suite, leaning against a pillar, watching her as she made her decision. 'It's a real bargain, Gil,' Casey assured him anxiously as he silently wrote a cheque and handed it over.

'Is it?' he asked carelessly. 'I was happy enough with the present arrangements.'

'There's nothing to stop you continuing with them,' she snapped. 'Personally I prefer a door on my bathroom.'

He shrugged. 'I'll send you a plumber on Monday to get started on the pipework.'

'How kind. But can I afford you?' she asked lightly.

'I'm sure I can work out suitable terms,' he replied, steering her firmly out of the showroom. 'In fact I think I might take a downpayment right now.' Instead of opening the car door as she had expected, he trapped her against its side, his hard body pressing against her.

'Gil!' she protested, but he seemed not to hear. For a moment she was mesmerised by the slow descent of his mouth to hers until a low ironic whistle from a youth loitering near by jerked her back to a sense of where she was. Gil straightened and opened the door.

'It'll keep,' he drawled. 'But I warn you, my interest rate is steep.' Blushing furiously, she ducked into her seat and stared straight ahead as Gil joined her, conscious that her breathing had become slightly ragged. He had been altogether too close to kissing her, and she had been altogether too close to letting him.

'I was going to look at kitchens while I was here,' she protested feebly as he started the car.

'Forget it, Casey. You've pushed your luck quite far enough for one day,' he said without expression. 'Besides, it's lunchtime.'

'Yes, my lord. Certainly, my lord,' she pretended to grovel. 'And what will your worship be wanting for his lunch today? A haunch of venison . . . jugged hare . . . a roast of swan, perhaps?'

'A sandwich will be quite adequate,

Casey. We're eating out this evening.'

'Oh? Where?'

'My first thought was the Old Bell. After all, it was where I proposed and it seemed appropriate — '

'No!' she said so emphatically that he turned to look at her, his mouth lifted in an ironic little smile.

'No? You didn't enjoy it?'

'I have absolutely no wish to be reminded of that particular occasion.'

'Just as well that I thought of something else, then, rather different. And much more fun.' And with that she had to be satisfied.

After lunch Gil suggested they finish clearing up the little boxroom. Casey agreed. 'If you've nothing else to do? No one to see?'

He eyed her with amusement. 'It's not my first choice of occupation, Catherine Mary Blake, you can be certain. But until you've discovered what Saturday afternoons are for it will help to keep me occupied.'

Casey curved her mouth into a

generous smile. 'I didn't realise that you wanted to go to the football match, Gil. Are Melchester at home this week?' she asked innocently. 'I'd be happy to go with you.'

He glanced at his watch. 'I don't think we'd make kick-off. Sorry. Next week, perhaps?'

'Lovely.' She looked at her hands. 'It's back to the wallpaper, then. Pity.' She glanced up in time to see him advancing on her in a manner that suggested it was time to make herself scarce. She flew up the stairs and by the time he caught up she was wielding her scraper with a determination that brooked no interruption.

★　★　★

'If you won't tell me where you're taking me,' Casey demanded as she stood in stockings and slip, her hands on her hips, 'the least you can do is suggest something suitable to wear.'

Gil shrugged. 'Nothing fancy.'

'Oh, thanks. That's a great help.' She flung open her wardrobe door. He leaned back against the bed, still wearing his bathrobe. She turned from him, concentrating on choosing a dress, painfully conscious of a desire to run her fingers through the damp mat of hair that curled on to his neck, to untie the belt fastening his robe and press herself against him.

'What happened to the little black number you wore to the Bell?' he asked. 'I'm sure that would go down very well.'

She kept her eyes firmly on her clothes. 'That would suggest that I'm going to be part of the entertainment. I'm beginning to like the sound of this less and less.'

'You didn't answer my question.'

'I sent it to a jumble sale,' she snapped.

'That's a shame.' He pushed himself off the bedpost and flicked through her clothes, pulling out a fine wool jersey dress in a glowing red, simply cut to show her figure off to perfection. 'This'll do.'

She took the hanger from him. 'If you wanted me to wear this, why didn't you just say so?' she asked.

'It was more fun the other way. I like to see you get mad. You get bright red patches on your cheekbones. Just here. And here.' He gently brushed each cheekbone with the tip of a thumb.

'They'll match the dress, then, won't they?' she said, stepping into it and turning to allow him to help her with the zip. He took his time, easing it up slowly, teasing her with his fingers along her spine all the way. He lifted aside the tendrils of hair that had escaped in curls around her nape when she had twisted it into a soft knot.

'Haven't you done it yet?' she asked impatiently.

'Not quite,' he murmured, his fingers still holding the delicate hook, keeping her captive, as he bent and placed a kiss on the nape of her neck. Before she could move he caught her around the waist and pulled her back against him, letting her feel his hard need of her.

'How does it feel, Casey, knowing that you do that to me?' he said thickly.

Frightened. She was frightened by the urgent need that she sensed in him. And frightened by the fragile nature of her determination not to respond, as a throbbing answer to his touch rippled through her. His hands slid upwards, seeking and finding, through the fine cloth of her dress, sensitive nipples already proud and longing for his touch. His lips touched her ear, and he whispered softly, 'Why don't you ask me to make love to you, Casey? You know you want me to.'

'No!' She twisted free, and turned on him, seeing a reflection of her own desire in the darkness of his eyes and the dull red patches colouring the hard bones of his cheeks. For a long moment they challenged one another, then Gil shrugged.

'You'd better wait for me downstairs. I won't be long.' He pushed her away and turned from her. She stood for a moment, not knowing whether she wanted to go, or stay and surrender totally, as he demanded. Then she turned and flew down the stairs.

A few minutes later he followed her. At the bottom of the stairs he paused. She had already thrown her black serape around her shoulders and was ready to leave. 'Will you be warm enough?' he asked, his voice hard, as he moved to the door. 'We're walking.'

'Far?' she asked, more concerned with the black high-heeled shoes she was wearing than any worry about the temperature.

'No. Not far.'

'I'll be fine.' It was a lovely late spring evening. At her parents' house the trees would be heavy with blossom. Even around the flat she had shared with Charlotte the air would be redolent with the scent of wallflowers. Here in this little backstreet there were no trees, no flowers, just hard pavements and parked cars.

The noise from the Carpenters' Arms in the next street reached out to them as they approached it. At the door Gil took her arm. 'This is it.'

He seemed to be waiting for her to protest, but she had no intention of giving him that satisfaction. 'How lovely.' She didn't wait for him to open the door, but pushed it open herself and led the way in.

It was crowded and smoky and she knew she was going to hate it, but come hell or high water she wasn't going to let it show. They pushed their way to the bar and Gil ordered drinks and told the barmaid to put them down for supper.

'What is it tonight?' he asked.

'Boiled beef and carrots with dumplings, Gil,' she said, taking his money. 'All right?'

He smiled his approval and led the way across to a group of people standing near the piano who greeted him warmly. 'Where's Dolly?' he asked, indicating the silent instrument. One of the men tore his eyes away from Casey long enough to answer him.

'On holiday. No music tonight. Aren't you going to introduce us?'

'Of course. Casey, let me introduce you to some old friends.' He whisked Casey through a list of names that she would never remember. He faltered when he came to the last of the group. She was small and dark and wearing a dress that Casey and Gil recognised at the same moment. Gil completed the introductions, taking care not to catch Casey's eye. 'Shame about the piano. This is Casey's first visit to the Carpenters'.'

'She'll be back next week.' Casey was conscious of an uncomfortable silence as if they didn't quite know what to make of her.

She cleared her throat. 'Perhaps I could play for a bit. What sort of thing does — er — Dolly play?' she offered.

'No, Casey, I don't think — '

But the stool was whisked out, the lid up and Casey was faced with a keyboard and no music. She considered the possibility of a little Chopin, put the idea down to a touch of hysteria and instead launched into a medley of Beatles' hits.

After that the requests came thick and fast. A lot she had never heard of, but she had played the piano for an old time music hall show at the Club and those tunes went down well.

Gil seemed to have disappeared, but a sudden parting of the crowd saw him in close conversation with the girl in the black dress. He was flirting outrageously and she was lapping it up. The girl slid on to his lap as Casey watched, her fingers continuing to play, finding the keys automatically, without any apparent help from her conscious brain. Gil seemed to sense her eyes on him and looked up. Quite deliberately he put his arm around the girl, pulled her close and bent to whisper something in her ear that made her laugh.

'Here's a drink, Casey.' The landlady placed a glass of orange juice on top of the piano. 'It's from Dave, over there.'

Casey turned to Dave, who waved and made a series of complicated gestures indicating his own glass and hers. Baffled by this display, she smiled and waved back and swallowed the juice, her throat dry from unaccustomed tobacco smoke. The crowd closed in again and she lost sight of Gil and the girl. The glasses of orange juice arrived in a steady stream and after a while she hardly noticed the odd little pain she was feeling somewhere in the region of her heart.

A sudden banging of a gong announced supper, and as she stood up to join the queue her legs felt a little rubbery. She picked up her cutlery and saw the girl in black behind her.

'I love your dress,' she said solemnly, then to her own surprise she giggled.

'Thanks.' The girl smoothed it over her hips. 'It was ever so expensive. But it's always worth paying for good clothes, don't you think?' she said, brazenly.

'Absolutely. And I'm sure fifty pence from the good as new stall made it just about the most expensive dress at the Brownie jumble.' Casey put her face close to the girl's suddenly rigid expression. 'And if you don't leave my husband alone I'll make sure everyone here knows exactly where you bought it,' she said silkily in her ear.

'You wouldn't!' But one look at Casey's face convinced her. She flushed scarlet and fled into the other bar.

Casey flopped in the vacant seat beside Gil. 'Your little friend seems to have deserted you.'

'I wonder why?' he said, amused.

'I've no idea.' She balanced her plate carefully on her knee and began to eat. 'But it makes me wonder, Gil. If you're so fond of dark, curvaceous women, why on earth did you bother with me?'

He paused, a forkful of food halfway to his mouth. 'Women? Plural?'

'She's the second gorgeous brunette I've seen you with your arm around this week.' She looked him straight in the eye.

'Is it indeed? Only two? I must be losing my touch.' His eyes glittered momentarily, then he shrugged carelessly. 'Perhaps it's a weakness of mine. Surely it doesn't worry you?' He met her eyes with a straight challenge.

'Damn you, Gil Blake.' She stood up, completely forgetting the plate, which slid from her lap, tipping its contents on the floor and landing upside-down on the carpet. She stared at it for a moment as if she wasn't quite sure where it had come from. 'I'm sorry.' She looked up, puzzled, as the landlady bustled over to clear up the mess.

'Don't you worry, dear.' She glanced at Gil's white face. 'I think you'd better take her home, Gil. She's had just a bit more than she's used to, I think.'

Gil looked at her closely. 'But she's been drinking orange juice.'

'Dave added a vodka. He really enjoyed her playing. I thought you knew.'

'Vodka! Dear heaven.' He looked at her more closely. 'It's my fault. I should have kept an eye on her. Sorry about the carpet.'

'It's nothing. Thanks for playing the piano, Casey. Come back soon.' Casey waved vaguely as a dozen or so voices called cheerio, and Gil tucked his arm firmly under hers as he led her outside.

The fresh air hit her like a sledge-hammer, and her knees buckled as they reached the corner. Gil swore and caught her up in his arms and carried her the rest of the way. He propped her up against the door as he hunted for his key, and she slid down on to the doorstep, giggling.

'I told her, you know,' she said, earnestly. 'I told her that I knew where she'd bought that dress.' She hiccuped. 'I said I'd tell everyone if she didn't scram.'

'Did you indeed?'

'Everybody was very kind. Kept buying me drinks. You didn't, Gil, 'cause you were busy. But I told her.'

He opened the door. 'Come on, you silly female . . . ' Then he stopped, because she couldn't hear him. He picked her up and stared down at her for a long moment, a smile of genuine amusement lifting his mouth. 'A jealous little puss, were we? Showed our claws?' He kissed her forehead and carried her inside.

* * *

There was a man with a jackhammer inside her head. She groaned and opened her eyes and then closed them quickly as the light burst in upon her brain.

'Casey.' The voice brooked no demur. With the utmost reluctance she opened them again. Gil was standing over her with a glass in his hand. 'Drink this,' he ordered.

She groaned once more, her hand to her head, and he watched, expressionless, as she struggled into a sitting position. She looked at the glass he held out to her and sniffed its contents suspiciously. 'What is it?' she asked, backing away.

'You don't want to know that. Just drink it. It'll help.'

'Nothing can help me,' she whispered. 'I'm dying.'

'No, you're not,' he said with a brisk lack of sympathy. 'You've got a hangover. Come on, drink this up.' He held the glass while she swallowed the liquid, tipping it up and not allowing her to leave a drop.

'Oh!' she shuddered. 'That was horrible.'

'Undoubtedly, but it'll make you feel better.'

She leaned back against the bed and covered her eyes. 'Could I have some water, do you think? And something for my head?'

'It might be arranged.' He made for the door, where he paused and looked back, his mouth curved in a mockery of a smile. 'Is there anything else I can bring you? A fried egg? Bacon? A couple of sausages?' he offered.

'Ohhh!' She slid under the bed-clothes and covered her head. A hangover? How on earth had she got a hangover? She tried to think straight. She remembered going to a pub where she had played the piano. She remembered that much. She'd been drinking orange juice. People had brought them and left them on top of the piano for her. They'd had something to eat . . . no, better not to think about food. Then? What then? She moaned. She'd obviously made a complete and utter fool of herself.

'Here you are.' Gil's voice was muffled.

'What is it?' she asked from under the quilt.

'If you don't come out, Casey, I'll come in after you,' he threatened.

Slowly she pulled down the covers. 'Are you very angry with me?' she asked, sheepishly.

He sat down on the bed and handed her a glass and a couple of tablets.

'Well, Casey. I have to say that after you'd tipped your supper over the floor . . . '

'I didn't!' One look at his face told her it was the truth. 'Oh, lord, I did.'

' . . . and I carried you home . . . ' She opened her mouth to protest and then closed it again. ' . . . I wasn't really feeling very charitable towards you. But . . . ' he grinned ' . . . then I undressed you and put you to bed, and I really enjoyed that.'

She looked down, anywhere but at the disconcerting expression in his eyes. 'You missed a button,' she said.

'So I did. My hands weren't very steady.' He leaned forward and remedied the situation.

Her own hands weren't very steady either and she needed both of them to hold on to the glass. She looked back up at his face. 'And then?' she challenged weakly.

'And then?' He grinned quite suddenly. 'And then, love, the sight of you suffering this morning has quite improved my temper.'

'I'm glad it amuses you,' she snapped, and winced at the sound of her own voice. 'I've never had a hangover before,' she finished in a whisper.

'It happens to everyone once. The trick is not to repeat the experience.'

'I certainly won't be drinking orange juice for a very long time,' she groaned, rubbing her eyes.

'I'm afraid Dave thought your playing deserved something rather stronger. It was the vodka in the orange juice that did the damage.'

She recalled the sign language. 'So that's what he meant!'

He took the glass from her. 'I think you're feeling a bit stronger already. You've stopped sounding humble.'

She considered this and had to agree. She didn't feel better, but she felt a little less ghastly. Tentatively she swung her legs to the floor and stood up. She swayed for a second and then steadied herself. 'I need the bathroom,' she said weakly.

Gil helped her into her dressing-gown and preceded her down the stairs. 'Don't lock the door. If you pass out I want to be able to get to you,' he warned.

She did as she was told and half an hour later, washed, dressed and with a cup of coffee inside her, she was beginning to feel almost human. Gil looked up from his newspaper.

'Anything you would like to do today? I had thought of lunch out, but — '

'Not a good idea,' Casey countered quickly.

'No,' he grinned wickedly. 'But I believe you could do with some fresh air. Fancy a walk down by the river?'

'That sounds . . . possible.'

'Come on, then.' He pulled her out of her chair. 'I'll get you a jacket.'

Ten minutes later Gil parked on the marina, and they walked slowly along, enjoying the boats and the youngsters from the sailing club tacking backwards and forwards for their Sunday morning lesson. The breeze across the river whipped some colour into her cheeks and soon, as Gil had predicted, Casey began to feel better. He tucked his arm firmly under hers and they walked together along the towpath. 'It's a long time since we did this, Casey. Do you remember?'

'I'm not likely to forget.'

'It must be nearly six years.'

'Five years, eight months, and three weeks,' she murmured.

Gil looked down at her, an odd little expression in his eyes. 'Didn't you count the days?' he asked.

She quickened her pace. Every day, every hour, every second. 'That would have been a little melodramatic, don't you think?' she replied, furious at betraying herself so carelessly.

'Especially once you had Michael to take your mind off . . . things.'

'Precisely.' She tried to pull away from him, but he held her close, and she didn't want to indulge in an unseemly struggle on the towpath. 'I don't suppose you went entirely uncomforted yourself,' she said crossly.

He smiled. 'Well, as you remarked yourself, I do have a weakness for shapely brunettes.' He looked up. 'Isn't that Annisgarth?'

'You know perfectly well it is.'

'I haven't had a chance to look at the finished works. Would you mind if we went up there?' he asked.

She did mind. She minded a great deal — Annisgarth was the last place on earth she wanted to go with Gil — but she didn't feel strong enough to make a fuss, and there was a determination about the set of his jaw that suggested it would be pointless anyway. She shrugged. 'I have a key if you want to go inside.'

6

'How generous of you. The last time I recall I was only offered a look through the window.'

She stared up at the sudden change in his voice. There was the hardness of slate about his eyes as he looked down at her, and the vein at his temple was throbbing angrily.

'But . . . ' she protested. He wasn't listening. He was already striding ahead of her and there was nothing she could do but follow, albeit reluctantly. Of course they couldn't go in that last time. The sale hadn't been completed — surely Gil must have realised that.

He was waiting impatiently at the front door and she handed him the key. 'Aren't you coming in?' he asked.

She shook her head. 'I'd rather not.'

'I think you ought to. It's hardly responsible to your client to let any old

Tom, Dick or Harry wander around unaccompanied.'

'But you're not any old . . . ' His expression was relentless and she sighed and led the way inside.

'Who is your client, by the way?'

'You don't know?' she asked, surprised. 'But you said O'Connor's did the alterations.'

'We were given our instructions by an architect acting for an offshore company.'

'Me too,' she said and he nodded absently, wandering through the house, looking out at the distant views, checking the work his own men had already done. 'I like this.' Gil indicated two smallish rooms knocked into one large drawing-room with windows on three sides looking over the garden to the gap in the hills that as a child she had thought was the sea.

'Yes. It worked very well,' she said dully. It was too painful. Casey didn't want to be here with Gil and she turned away, anxious to leave, but he was checking the new central-heating system.

'It's time the place was done up. It was beginning to deteriorate.' There was an implied criticism in his voice that jarred.

'Dad let it to a local company until recently. It was too big for me . . . '

'Much,' he agreed. 'It was for you when you married. I remember.' Gil stood and looked out across the valley. 'It's going to be lovely, Casey. Your father should never have taken it from you. It was an act of desperation; he must have known it would never be enough to save him.'

'I suppose he did,' Casey admitted. 'But I pushed him into it. I think perhaps I was more desperate than he was.'

'I see.'

Her headache had returned and she shivered slightly in a chill that had little to do with the weather. 'Let's go, Gil. It was a mistake to come here with you.' She waited until he joined her on the step and closed the front door with a bang.

'You brought me up here once before to look at the house. Do you remember that day, Casey?'

She didn't answer because she couldn't. Instead she ran blindly for the woods, ignoring his shout, stopping only when she'd reached the shelter of the trees. Weak and dizzy, she slumped on the ground under their shelter. Of course she remembered that day. How could she ever forget? She had been young and in love and had brought Gil to see her house, expecting him to fall in love with it as she had.

She had wanted him to know that there was no barrier to marriage between them. Her mother would fret, she had a society wedding in mind, but she had her house and they could live there and be happy ever after. What a stupid, naive little fool she had been.

She had been just a week short of her eighteenth birthday, and she had a dream. She had made a picnic and brought Gil up to the wood to give it a chance to become reality.

They had eaten and were sitting quietly against the massive bole of a tree, finishing a bottle of wine. 'It's my birthday next week. I'm having a party at the Club. Will you come?' she asked a little shyly.

'I don't think so. Mummy wouldn't like it, would she? And caddies are never allowed into the clubhouse.'

'You're a caddy?' she exclaimed with amusement. 'I've never seen you.'

'I used to be. After school. Not for a long time. We'll have a private celebration,' he murmured, leaning across to kiss her, 'just you and me.' She didn't persist; the party didn't matter. There was something far more important. She jumped up and held out her hand.

'Come on, Gil. I want to show you something. It's my birthday present from Dad.'

He followed her to the edge of the wood and stared across the open meadow, shading his eyes against the sun.

'There. My house.' She turned to

him, hoping he would see now what she was trying to say.

'But it's huge. Whatever do you want a house like that for?' he asked, his eyes suddenly narrow.

She knew she had gone pink. 'It's for when I get married.' The words were out now and she waited, breathless, wanting him to ask her.

'You're going to live here, when you get married?' he echoed her words.

'Yes. Dad got the lady who lived there to give him first refusal ages ago, and now she's getting too old to live by herself so she's gone to live in a home.' She tugged his hand impatiently. 'Tomorrow it will be mine. That's when the contracts will be signed. Come and look,' she urged. 'Not inside, but you can see through the windows.'

He resisted her urging. 'No!' He turned sharply and pulled her after him back into the darkness of the woods, into the moss-lined dell hidden in the tall summer bracken. 'I'm not interested in an old house, Casey O'Connor.

I'm only interested in you.' He pulled her down beside him and rolled over, pinning her beneath him, wrapping a handful of her long hair around his fist and holding her fast.

She laughed, delighting in the power she had over a man six years her senior, and experienced in the ways of the world in which she was just a beginner.

His kiss, gentle, teasing, cut off her laughter and she responded with pleasure, enjoying the weight of his body on hers, twining her fingers through his overlong jet curls, capturing him in turn, as his urgency fired a new, hungering sensation deep inside her. Her lips parted to allow him to explore the depths of her mouth, and even as his tongue probed, explored, teased, she knew that it was never going to be enough.

Her hands strayed down his back and, finding the gap where his T-shirt had pulled free from his jeans, slid up inside, roving his hard body, making it her own. The tips of her fingers stroked warm skin, revelling in the feel of his muscles rippling under her touch. He raised his head and his expression was triumphant as he saw her pupils darkly dilated with a passion that echoed his own.

'Casey.' He breathed her name as his hand worked free the buttons of her blouse, and she arched brazenly towards him as his teeth grazed her nipples, gasping as he drew one hungrily into his mouth. Her hands needed to touch him, to feel the driving urgency that was igniting her, making her skin burn so that she wanted to tear away her clothes. But he was doing that for her. She raised her hips so that he could ease away her jeans, crying out as his hand touched the soft warm place where she longed to feel him, until she was lost in a pitch of pleasure that she had not dreamed was possible. And then he was above her, poised to make her a woman. His woman.

'Remember this, Casey,' Gil whispered, his voice hoarse with desire. 'Remember this when you're married and living in your old house with the sort of man that rich girls marry. Remember this.'

Casey stared up at him. His words had hit her like a cold pail of water, bringing her savagely back to earth, and making her only too aware of where she was and what was happening.

'No!' Her voice rang out and drove the collared doves in noisy panic from their perches in the trees above them. 'No!' She placed her hands hard against his chest and pushed, rolling clear and staggering to her feet. She grabbed her clothes, struggling into them in frenzied desperation, as Gil had roared his angry frustration. She ignored the tears that were pouring down her cheeks in her need to get away from him.

She had brought him there to show him her house, hoping that he would want to share it with her. But he hadn't wanted that. And his words had made it quite clear that there was to be no future for them. He had pursued the boss's daughter to surrender-point.

That had been all he had wanted. And she knew what building sites were like. They were probably running a book on how long it would be before she succumbed.

He had dressed as quickly as she had and was advancing towards her, his face white and angry. 'Casey, listen . . . ' As he caught her arm she tried to pull away.

'Don't touch me!' she cried, but he took no notice and in desperation she threatened him. 'If you lay one finger on me again, Gil Blake, I'll have you sacked! I'll have you sacked anyway!'

It had been enough. He had stopped in his tracks, his face like stone, and his arm dropped to his side. For a moment she had stayed there, fixed by the red-hot anger in his eyes. Then she had turned and run. She had run home and hidden herself away in her room, calling herself every kind of a fool, and she had stayed there until there were no more tears to shed and she felt quite cold and empty.

She had gone to college, glad to get away, and when she returned with her diploma, ready to work in her father's drawing office, there had been Michael.

But Michael had never had the power to drive Gil from her mind. She had returned to this spot time and time again to relive the moment. And each time she remembered it the wish was stronger. The wish that she had taken the moment offered by Gil. That she had such a memory to cherish. Even if the love had been all on her side, it would have been enough.

'Still running, Casey?' She looked up. Gil was standing over her. For a moment the sense of *déjà vu* was so strong that she expected him to pull her to her feet and draw her into the woods as he had done before. But he made no move towards her.

Instead she stood up and brushed the dried leaves from her trousers. 'No. I've stopped running, Gil.' She shivered.

He stared around him. 'I couldn't say how many times I've dreamed about this place. It hasn't changed at all.'

'No. It hasn't changed.'

He tore his eyes from her and stared up at the sky. 'It's going to rain,' he said, abruptly. 'We'd better get home.' He wrapped his arm around her and they half ran back to the car, the sudden downpour catching them on the towpath, soaking them through before they got to the car. They drove silently back through the wet town and for the first time Casey was truly glad to get back to her little house.

Gil put a light to the fire already laid in the grate while she put on the kettle. He followed her into the kitchen with a towel, which he draped over her hair and she leaned against him, enjoying the vigorous towelling.

'Go and get changed, Casey. You'll catch a chill.' His voice was hoarse.

'Actually, Gil . . . ' She turned to face him. 'I . . . I think I'd like a bath first.' She felt herself going pink under his careful scrutiny.

'Are you sure?'

'Absolutely.'

He nodded carefully. 'I'll fetch it in. But go and get out of those wet things.'

She ran lightly up the stairs. The decision made, she felt at peace with herself. She stripped off her wet clothes and wrapped herself in her towelling robe. She didn't hurry. For a while she sat in front of the dressing-table and examined her reflection.

She had been a fool. No matter what his motives Gil had come back to her. She had wanted him to say that love had brought him back. But suddenly it didn't matter; her pride was nothing. If it was revenge he wanted he was going to be thwarted because she still wanted him, had never stopped wanting him. She pulled a brush through her damp hair. If it was revenge he wanted he should never have made her marry him. His presence hadn't brought her pain. It was her own rejection of him that had done that. She touched her lips, remembering the promise of his kiss on their wedding-day, and she smiled.

As she stood up and tightened the belt around her narrow waist she heard a phone ring. With an irritated shake of her head she hurried down the stairs, but Gil had already answered and she paused at the foot of the stairs as he spoke quietly into the receiver of a portable telephone that she had never seen before. 'I told you not to ring me here,' he said quietly, his back to her. 'I don't care what . . . ' Casey listened, hardly believing her ears as he continued. 'Yes, it is a bad time. The worst possible time . . . No, no, darling, I'll come straight away . . . It's just . . . ' He turned and saw her standing at the foot of the stairs. 'Give me twenty minutes.' He flicked the phone closed as she stepped down into the room. 'Casey . . . I have to go out.'

'Yes. So I heard. Please don't let me detain you.'

'It's business. I wouldn't go, but . . . ' Ice water drained through her at his blatant lie, and she instinctively pulled her robe closer about her, rubbing her arms to try to warm them.

'Brunette business?' she challenged him. 'The sort of business called 'darling'?' He made a move towards her but she put out a hand to stop him. 'Please don't try to make excuses. I couldn't bear it. Just go.'

'Darling?' He shook his head. 'No, Casey, it's not what you think.' He threw a desperate glance at his watch. 'I haven't got time to explain.'

'There's nothing to explain, Gil.'

'That's the point,' he asserted, then he threw his hands up in the air. 'Damn!' Without another word he turned and left.

Casey leaned towards the fire, holding herself tightly, rocking gently in an effort to soothe the hurt that jabbed through her. 'He'll catch his death of cold in those wet clothes,' she complained to the cat, who had clearly been caught in the open when it rained. In reply she extended a rear leg elegantly and began to lick it dry.

It seemed stupid to waste the bath.

She soaked some heat back into her bones, then emptied it in the back yard. She prowled about the house, unable to settle, and her movement began to affect the cat, who seemed restless and fidgety.

Once she started to dial Charlotte's number. But what could she say? Married a week and at a loose end on Sunday afternoon? No. Pride demanded that she lick her wounds in private.

She caught herself putting the kettle on for want of something to do. Furious with herself, she grabbed her bag and left the house. She started the van and drove away without thought of where she would go, just knowing that she had to escape from the powerful presence of Gil that, even when he wasn't there, seemed to brood in every corner of the house.

Casey pulled over finally in a lay-by that looked out over the hills rolling away towards Oxford, but she closed her eyes to the scenery before her.

She had come so close to surrender. And how confident he must be that she would eventually succumb, to go racing away to another woman at the moment of his triumph. She blinked furiously, refusing to cry. She had cried too many tears over Gil Blake. She had no choice but to share his house, and that barren bed with the unsheathed sword of pride between them. But pride was all she had left. Until he relented and let her go it would have to be enough.

Someone had set up a stall selling plants at the far end of the lay-by and she stopped, attracted by the bright colours. There were some pots of pansies, bright yellow and white. On a sudden impulse she bought them, and stood them where she could see them from the kitchen window. ''And there is pansies, that's for thoughts . . .'' she murmured, and turned away, hating hers.

Misery finally drove her upstairs to bed. She didn't bother with the main light, and as she walked across to turn on the side light a noise from the bed froze her in her tracks. A movement of something white there made the hairs rise on the nape of her neck. Then with sudden relief she recognised the crooning sound. She snapped on the light and the cat purred softly up at her.

'Well, who's been a clever girl, then?' Casey said, and counted the kittens. 'Five of them. And from the look of that little ginger job I needn't ask who the father is, need I?' The cat licked her kittens, purring loudly. 'Well, that puts my sleeping arrangements in a bit of a bother.' The cat looked at her anxiously. 'No. I won't move you tonight.' She gathered her pyjamas and some blankets from the top of the wardrobe and switched off the light.

Downstairs she banked up the fire and wrote a note for Gil, warning him to stay out of the bedroom. She wrapped herself in a blanket and tried to sleep, but cars continually came down the road and parked. Each time a door banged she started, sure that this time it must be Gil.

Finally she threw off the blanket and warmed some milk. Wondering if the cat would like a drink, she poured some into a bowl and carried it upstairs. She put on the small light and showed it to the cat, who lapped it greedily while she held the dish.

A car door banged and she started, almost spilling the milk when she heard Gil's key slide into the lock. The cat was still lapping and Casey couldn't move until she had finished. But she didn't need to rush down. Gil burst into the room, his face dark with anger, her note in his hand.

'What the hell is this?' he demanded furiously, waving it at her. And then he stopped as he took in the scene before him. Casey stood up. 'I'm afraid our bed is otherwise occupied for tonight,' she apologised. 'I'll move her in the morning.'

'I thought . . . ' He ran a hand distractedly through his hair.

'Yes?'

'I thought this was a reaction to . . . earlier.'

She took the note and read it: ' 'PLEASE KEEP OUT OF THE BEDROOM'. What's wrong with that? I thought I might be asleep when you came in. I didn't want you barging up here disturbing her.'

'And that's exactly what I did, because you were up here.' He had dark circles under his eyes, she noticed. 'I thought that was why you didn't want me to come up.'

Light dawned. 'It doesn't do to jump to conclusions, Gil. Come on. Let's leave her in peace.' She turned off the light and he followed her down the stairs. The damp clothes he had gone out in had been replaced by a dark suit and fresh striped shirt. He saw her look and glanced down.

'I keep a change of clothes at the office.'

'At the office?' she remarked drily. 'Very convenient. And a razor?'

He ignored the question. 'I thought

you just said something about not jumping to conclusions?' he reminded her.

'I'm not jumping, Gil. I'm walking very slowly. But the conclusions come out about the same. You married me as some sort of perverse revenge for what you think I did to you. Believe me, I regretted it, still regret it, even though I know I was right. That should be revenge enough for you.' Her eyes widened in appeal. 'Would it be so hard to put an end to this charade? Now.'

His eyes glowed dully. 'You shouldn't have had me sacked, Casey. It was an abuse of power.'

She drew her brows together in confusion. 'I never had you sacked, Gil. I never told anyone about the game you were playing with me.'

'Game?' He brushed the word away with an angry gesture. 'Don't lie to me, Casey. I still have the letter. Not that I was planning on staying. I went to the office on Monday morning to tell them I was leaving, and it was waiting for me, with my cards and a cheque. Your father's personal cheque. Rather too much money for any mistake in the matter.'

'A cheque?' She felt herself colouring. 'I see. So that's how you got started in business. Perhaps you should be thanking Dad, instead of — '

'See!' he furiously interrupted. 'You see nothing, Casey! I tore up his damn cheque. I didn't want his filthy money. But I kept the letter. And whenever I felt the anger getting just a little bit dull I took it out and sharpened it up on the words. That's what got me started, not your father's money!'

She stood up, her face stiff with shame at what she and her father had done to him. 'How you must hate me,' she said.

He took a step towards her. 'I — '

'If you're hungry there's some cold chicken in the fridge,' she said to stop him. Anything to stop him saying the words out loud.

He took a deep steadying breath and

turned away. 'I've already eaten.'

'Of course you have.' With the little brunette no doubt. 'Goodnight, Gil.'

'Casey!' he protested, striding angrily towards her, but she drew her dressing-gown more tightly around her, picked up her blanket and held it like a shield between them.

'I'll sleep in the attic,' she said, surprised at the calm even voice that did not seem to quite belong to her.

'And where am I supposed to sleep?' he demanded.

'Why don't you use the office?' she suggested coolly. 'It seems to have every amenity.'

She turned away then so that he shouldn't see the tears sliding down her cheeks, and walked heavily up the two flights of stairs to the attic. She heard him coming up behind her, and held her breath, but he didn't follow her to the top of the house. As she lay curled in a cold sleepless huddle she heard him moving about for a while. But she must have finally slept. There was a grey light filtering through the window when his footstep on the stairs woke her.

'Casey?' he called softly.

She kept her eyes closed and didn't move. He called once more and, after a slight pause, went back down. A few moments later she heard the front door being quietly closed and the car starting and being driven away down the road. Only then did she straighten her stiff limbs.

In the sitting-room Gil's blanket was folded neatly, the fire was relaid and on the small table there was a note. With trembling fingers she opened it.

Don't forget we have a dinner party tomorrow. I'll try and get home before our guests arrive. Gil.

And there was a letter. It was old and yellowed, the creases split and worn. Casey opened it slowly. It was the O'Connor company letterhead, and the letter politely told Gil that his services were no longer required. Nothing extraordinary. Nothing to show that it was anything more than what it seemed. A straightforward dismissal. Except that Gil had said there had been a personal cheque enclosed. A large cheque.

She looked at it again. And her eyes narrowed.

'Oh, Mother!' she whispered. 'How could you?' The letter was signed 'J O'Connor' without doubt. But the 'J' was for June, not James. That was why it had been a personal cheque. Her father had never known and somehow that made things seem a little better. Or perhaps a little worse. She wasn't quite sure. But on reflection, she decided with a wry smile, her father's reaction would have been very different. If he had found out what had happened in the wood he would have produced his shotgun and demanded a wedding. It wouldn't have worried him one jot that Gil wasn't on the social register.

She sank slowly into an armchair.

Not that it made any difference now. She looked again at Gil's note. He had taken her at her word and moved out. And this time she would be the one who would have to go away. She owed the people who worked there, whose lives were tied up with O'Connor's, that much.

Not immediately, of course. They would play at being married for the sake of appearances for a while, but Gil couldn't leave Melchester now that he owned the company.

Something of Gil's need to go so far away was suddenly very clear to her. Apart, Melchester was not big enough to hold them both.

She picked the milk up from the doorstep and returned a friendly wave from her neighbour opposite. In the scullery she found the cat and kittens contentedly tucked into a box with an old towel in the bottom and she wondered what had happened to the quilt.

All day she pondered on the way it

was possible to carry on with your life when your heart was breaking.

The promised plumber turned up to install the pipework for the bathroom and she managed to keep up a cheerful chatter with him. She planned the food for the dinner party and she shone the house until there was nothing left to polish. But the pain stayed, a constant aching regret for something that might have been, but had never really had a chance.

7

All Monday Casey worked with an ear tuned for the telephone, hoping that Gil would ring, and furious with herself for hoping. After the sixth false alarm when she had picked it up to find a supplier with a query, or a contractor hoping for work, she went out and left the phone behind.

A check on Gil's wardrobe showed that he had taken an overnight bag, nothing more. His note had said he would return for the dinner party and she had to accept that and get on as best she could. But the bed that she had longed to sleep in by herself was strangely cold and empty without him and she found sleep elusive.

She spent Tuesday morning rearranging the living-room in order to get the kitchen table in. She had covered it with a thick cloth to disguise its humble nature, laid it and placed a small bowl of flowers in the centre, when the plumber arrived with the bathroom suite.

She stared in amazement at the lorry and the men waiting to offload. 'You can't! Not now!'

'Mr Blake's orders, ma'am.' His mate nodded. 'He left word yesterday that it had to be fitted by this evening.'

'Mr Blake?' He couldn't telephone her, but he could find time to talk to plumbers. Colour touched her cheekbones with a dangerous pink. 'In that case, please come in.' She stood aside and watched as they tramped their boots across her newly cleaned carpet and up the stairs. She promised herself a word with Mr Blake about his sense of timing when he did turn up.

Unable to bear to watch the mounting chaos, she retired to the kitchen and carried on with the preparations for the meal. Then she left the men still banging upstairs, and went to have her hair done.

By the time she returned the plumbers had gone and the suite was installed. Despite the upheaval Casey was pleased. She touched the gleaming white porcelain, allowing herself to imagine the pleasure of a soak in hot suds that didn't have to be emptied in the yard. She gave the mahogany panels a loving polish and promised herself a proper bath, once she had returned the living-room to its pristine condition.

By half-past six there was nothing left to do. Casey placed the plug in the bath and turned on the taps, watching with satisfaction as the steaming water gushed in. She added bath salts and with a glance at her watch rationed herself to fifteen minutes of total luxury. She had been immersed for no more than two minutes when the phone rang, and the phone was downstairs.

She was certain it was Gil. The timing was too perfect to be anyone else. Half angry, half amused, she leapt out and, swathed in a towel, ran downstairs.

'Gil?' she answered.

'Mrs Blake? This is Darlene Forster.' Casey's nerves gave a sudden jerk at the harsh Australian twang.

'Darlene Forster?'

'Gil's PA. He telephoned and asked me to check that the bathroom had been fitted satisfactorily, and he said to remind you that the bath shouldn't be used for twenty-four hours. I've no idea why.'

'Darlene?' Casey breathed. 'That's an uncommon name.'

The woman laughed. 'Not back home in Australia, Mrs Blake.' She paused. 'Did your bathroom get fitted?'

'Oh, yes. Thank you. It's fine, I was just having a . . . ' Casey stared at the phone in horror. 'Not use it for twenty-four hours?'

'That's right. Is it something to do with the putty stuff the plumbers use?'

'I expect so, Mrs Forster. Thanks for phoning.'

'Call me Darlene, please. Oh, and Gil said to tell you he'll be a bit on the late side, but he will be there.'

'Oh, I see. Well, thanks again.' She put down the phone and slowly walked back up the stairs. Darlene? Darling? Could she have misheard? Twice? For a long moment she stared at the bath. Then furiously she pulled the plug. 'So much for modern plumbing,' she said bitterly and went to dress for her guests.

She had decided on a pair of softly gathered silk trousers in her favourite turquoise and a matching top in turquoise and amethyst, and she fastened a pair of amethyst and gold studs to her ears. Then she slipped Gil's diamond on to her finger. Tonight, at least, they would put on a show for the world as the perfect married couple.

Downstairs she put a match to the fire, turned on the lamps and went to check on her food in the kitchen. A knock on the door promptly at seven-thirty heralded the first arrival.

'Casey! This is so quaint!'

Casey winced inwardly but smiled a welcome. 'Glad you like it, Alison. Hello, Mike. Come on in and have a drink.'

The couple looked around them and Casey saw them exchange a glance. She had deliberately chosen to invite them, knowing they would absorb every detail and pass it along. At least that way it would all be a nine-days' wonder and then forgotten. She hoped.

She poured them drinks and answered the door to another knock. To her relief it was Charlotte. She brought a pile of post and a warm hug.

'A real fire. How lovely!' she exclaimed, stretching out her hands to it. She took her drink and immediately engaged Alison and Mike in small talk, keeping them firmly on the safe subject of business.

Another knock brought their last three guests, who hid their surprise at her surroundings under well bred politeness.

'Gil is a little late, I'm afraid,' Casey

told them. 'Business.'

She had just decided that the food couldn't wait any longer and had gone through to the kitchen with Charlotte when they heard Gil's key slide into the lock. 'You leave this to me,' Charlotte urged, and pushed Casey out of the kitchen.

She hardly knew how to greet her husband in public. They had parted in anger but with the eyes of these people on her she knew she must put a brave face on things. She wondered uneasily if they would expect her to throw her arms around him. Indecision deserted her the moment she set eyes on him.

'Gilliam Blake!' she exploded.

He paused in the act of removing a pair of mud-caked boots. He was wearing denim dungarees thickly encrusted with concrete and his black hair was whitened with the same substance.

'Sorry. Should I have gone around the back?' His eyes sparkled as they took in the casual elegance of his guests, and the table laid with heavy silver on a snowy cloth.

She bit back an acid comment and forced a warm smile. 'Don't be silly.' She walked over to him, planning to link her arm with his. One look at his shirt changed her mind.

'I had a bit of bother with a concrete mixer,' he explained to their bemused guests. 'And you can't leave it. If the concrete goes off in the drum it's a nightmare.' His boots held in one hand, he advanced into the room and, with silent laughter creasing his eyes, he bent and kissed Casey full on the lips. 'Forget dinner,' he drawled. 'I'll eat you instead.'

'Not dressed like that, you won't!'

'Spoilsport. Did the bathroom come?'

'I'm sure *Darlene* told you it did!' she hissed, only too aware that Gil was quite deliberately offering them both up as entertainment for her friends.

'I'll be right down.' He grinned, and dropped a kiss on her nose before disappearing up the stairs. She turned to offer her guests another drink while they were waiting, and went bright pink as she realised that she was the object of every eye.

'Young love is a wonderful thing,' Alison said with tolerant amusement, as she accepted a glass of wine.

Gil reappeared in less than fifteen minutes, immaculate in light grey trousers teamed with a darker grey shirt striped in burgundy and a matching plain burgundy tie.

Formal introductions were made but Gil paused when he reached Charlotte. 'We've met before, haven't we?'

'I was Casey's bridesmaid. Charlotte Spearing.'

'So you were. Charlotte? You and Casey shared a flat, didn't you?'

'That's right. But please call me Charlie. Everyone does.'

Gil raised his eyes to Casey. 'This is Charlie?'

Casey smiled innocently. 'Didn't I say?' She carried on with the introductions. Gil shook hands firmly with the men and flirted outrageously with the women, raising their hands to his lips. Casey watched helplessly as he had everyone eating out of his hand within minutes.

'Did I hear you say you've had a new bathroom fitted?' Casey heard someone ask him.

'Yes,' he said, glancing across at her. 'She didn't much like the tin job in front of the fire, more's the pity.' Then, seeing the blank expression this statement produced, 'The house didn't have a bathroom when we moved in,' he explained.

'Good heavens!'

'Hasn't Casey given you the grand tour?' he asked in surprise.

'Not yet,' Casey cut in, passing around the plates.

'Oh, great. Asparagus.' He handed the sauce to Charlotte. 'Of course, she's only just started to do the place up. Well, it's only been eleven days, and we've been . . . busy.' He leaned over and picked up her hand, kissing the fingertips. She would have snatched them away but his hold was deceptively firm. 'Haven't we, darling?' He stressed the endearment.

'Very.'

'Not too busy to help with the rose ball, I hope,' Alison interrupted.

'Rose ball?' Gil enquired, looking from one to the other.

'A charity thing we have at the Club in June. Casey and her mother always organise the decorations.'

'I'm not sure about this year. Mother is away — '

'Oh, yes,' Gil interrupted. 'I remember. My mother always used to help, too.' He grinned at their polite enquiring faces. 'In the kitchen.'

'And Mrs Hetherington is chairwoman,' Casey dropped hastily into the sudden silence, and with a finality that she hoped would close the subject.

Alison was the first to recover her voice. 'You can't avoid one another forever, Casey. Especially now Gil is a member. Better get it over and done with.'

'I think Casey is suggesting that Mrs Hetherington may not want her,' Charlotte intervened, as Casey was reduced to open-mouthed speechlessness at this stunning piece of news. The waiting list for membership of Melchester Golf and Country Club was years long.

The conversation continued around her. 'You think she's got so much talented help that she can be choosy? She'll want her year as chairwoman to be the best ever, and for that she needs Casey. Whether she likes it or not.'

'Say you'll do it,' Alison pressed.

Casey looked at Gil. 'I think you should, sweetheart,' he murmured, refusing to meet her eye. 'Must keep up the family traditions.'

Casey swallowed hard. 'If Mrs Hetherington asks, then of course I'll be glad to help.'

Charlotte helped her to clear the plates and walked into the kitchen. 'Casey!'

Casey arrived to find her standing staring up at the light fitting, from which a steady drip was forming a pool of water on the floor.

'Damn!'

'Whatever shall we do?' Charlotte whispered.

'How about leaving quietly by the back door?' Casey suggested.

'This isn't the time for joking!' Charlotte giggled under cover of a burst of laughter from the living-room.

'Who's joking?' Casey said bitterly. 'But there's nothing we can do. Let's get the food out of here while we've still got some light.' The words were barely out of her mouth before the fuse blew and the kitchen plunged into darkness.

Gil appeared in the doorway, a candle from the table casting a dim light into the kitchen. He lifted the candle to survey the wrecked light fitting. 'Will dinner wait while I fix the fuse, or can we carry on by candle-light?' he asked casually.

'Leave the candle and we can manage,' Casey said quickly, aware that the tone of his voice was deceptive. Gil knew very well what had happened and she would be hearing from him as soon as they were alone. 'Good job it's a gas cooker,' she added.

'Probably,' was his only retort, but he left the candle and returned to their guests.

It was late when they closed the door on the last of their visitors and Casey leaned against it, surveying the wreck of the feast in the guttering light of the candles.

'I'll fix the fuse,' Gil said.

'There's no need. We've plenty of candles. I'll do it in the morning.'

'What about the freezer?'

'Still working. It's on a different circuit. Only the lights went.'

'That's all right, then.' There was a pause. 'Didn't Darlene pass on my message about not using the bath?'

'She telephoned, but it was too late.' She looked at him to find that he was laughing at her. 'I am sorry.'

'Never mind. The wiring needs

checking over. This will be as good a time as any. How about a brandy to see us to bed?'

'You're staying, then?' she asked, surprised.

'Staying? Of course I'm staying. Where would I be going at this time of night?'

'Why don't you tell me? Perhaps the same place you slept last night?'

'I had a series of meetings in London and I knew they would go on late so I stayed in town.' He poured two glasses of brandy and handed one to her. 'You could have phoned the office if you needed me. Darlene Forster always knows where I am.'

'I'll bet!'

He was amused by her irritation. 'I would have told you myself, but you were asleep when I came up to the attic and I didn't want to wake you.' He looked up. 'You'd had a disturbed night what with one thing and another. How are the kittens, by the way?'

'Fine.'

'I've got the quilt in the car. Darlene took it to be cleaned.'

'She's quite a treasure. And the hours she puts in; she must be worth her weight in gold-plated taps,' Casey snapped.

'She is. Good-looking, too. Dark, curvaceous. You know how I go for the type.' Casey felt her fingers curl into angry claws as she remembered Gil getting into the lift at the Melchester Hotel. So that was Darlene. Gil grinned at her. 'Here.' He handed her a glass and stretched out in front of the dying embers of the fire. 'It was a successful evening, wouldn't you say?'

'Oh, yes. The details of our 'bijou' residence will be all around Melchester by lunchtime tomorrow.' She sipped her drink and regarded the man she had married by the flickering light from the fire. He looked tired. Whatever he had been doing in London had been hard work and Casey realised just how little she knew about him. Only what he had told her himself about the way he had built up a business from scratch.

But when her father owned the company he had never found it necessary to have late business meetings in London. He returned her look.

'What?' he asked, as if he could sense the questions on her mind.

'I was just wondering about the site foreman routine that we were treated to when you came home,' she hedged.

He laughed and suddenly the tiredness fell from his face. 'Fun, wasn't it? You should have seen your face. But there really was a problem with a mixer, and we were halfway through a major concrete pour. One of the men loaned me some clothes and we managed to keep it going.'

'Heroic,' she teased, but pleased by the image of a sweating, muscle-straining Gil. So much more like the man she had fallen in love with.

'I was going to have a shower and change back into the suit, but somehow I just couldn't resist putting on a performance. Were they impressed, do you think?'

'Quite overcome. Good job they've already invited you to join the Club, or that little performance might have cost you dear.'

'Do you think so? After your father put in a good word for me?'

'My father waited four years to become a member, if memory serves me correctly, and even then it was my mother's charity works that finally got him admitted,' Casey said, suddenly sick of the game they were playing. 'I don't know how you swung it, Gil, but I know that it would take more than a good word from Dad to get you past the waiting list. I'm going to bed.' She stood up. 'Don't forget to bring the quilt up when you come. I missed it.'

He half rose and she stood defiantly at the foot of the stairs, challenging him to follow through and carry her up the stairs the way he had done that first day, and make her truly his wife. For a moment, a brief heart-stopping moment, she thought he was going to do just that.

'Ask me, Casey,' he said softly, his eyes dark pools in the firelight. 'Ask me very nicely.' They both knew that the quilt was an irrelevance. It had nothing to do with what made the air jump and crackle between them. Casey stood mesmerised, unable to advance or retreat. 'Ask me!' he demanded, his voice harsh and shocking in the little room.

'No!' Even as the word was wrenched from her she regretted it, but it was too late to recall, and Gil subsided into the armchair, his eyes already returned to the embers.

'Goodnight, Casey.' It was a dismissal. Reluctantly she turned and mounted the stairs, but although she lay awake for hours he did not follow her.

★　★　★

'Casey Blake.'

'Casey. My dear.' Mrs Hetherington's voice echoed condescendingly from the other end of the telephone. 'How are you?' Casey's heart sank. It had been days since the dinner party and she had hoped that Michael's mother had vetoed her involvement in the arrangements for the rose ball.

'Very well, thank you. And you?'

'Fine.'

There was an awkward pause as Casey considered whether she should ask how Michael was, but before she could do so Mrs Hetherington had launched herself into the carefully worded request for assistance. 'I realise,' she concluded, 'that this is a little awkward for both of us, but we're both grown women and it would be ridiculous to let this unfortunate affair destroy such a long-standing family friendship. Michael has taken it very well on the whole. He was shocked, of course. But I told him that any girl's head might be turned . . . '

'Turned?' Casey gasped.

Mrs Hetherington might not have paused ' . . . and so much better *before* you had made the mistake of marrying him. He has quite come to terms with the situation.'

Casey listened to this sting in the tail and realised that, however much she deserved the veiled rebuke, no one deserved the wretched woman for a mother-in-law.

'Of course, I'll be happy to help, Mrs Hetherington. I know Mother would want me to.'

'We're having a meeting this afternoon. I realise it's short notice — '

'No problem,' she interrupted. It was a bit like the dentist: the less time to think about it the better. She made a note of the time and hung up.

'Had my head turned?' she asked the telephone before putting it back on her desk. 'Turned by what?' Then the phone began to ring again and for a while work drove all other thoughts to the back of her mind.

Despite her assurance that the short notice for the meeting was no problem, Casey found that a flurry of last-minute phone calls left her on the borderline of late. She banged the front door behind her and found herself facing a flat tyre with no time to change it.

'Blast!' She pulled the phone out of her bag and jabbed in the number of the local taxi company. She arrived late, breathed her apologies, and dived into the meeting which had already begun.

Mrs Hetherington believed in stately committee meetings. It was two hours before a theme had been agreed upon, responsibilities divided and proceedings could be brought to a satisfactory conclusion. 'A glass of sherry is in order, I think,' Mrs Hetherington beamed.

Casey checked her watch. 'Would you mind if I just phoned for a taxi?'

'No, dear. Help yourself. You know where the phone is.'

Casey had intended to use her own telephone, but welcomed the opportunity to escape the overpowering politeness of her hostess for a moment. In the hall she picked up the receiver and took a moment to recall the number of the taxi rank. As she stood there the front door swung open and Michael stood, open-mouthed, in the doorway.

'Casey!'

'Hello, Michael.'

'What on earth . . . ?'

'Rose ball.'

She found herself smiling at the shorthand conversation of two people who had been close friends for a long time.

'It's good to see you, Casey. Are you well?' He took her hand and looked at her anxiously. 'You've lost weight.'

'I've been busy.' She indicated the phone. 'I'm just calling a taxi. I had a flat tyre.'

'Don't do that. I'll run you home.'

'I don't think — '

'Please, Casey.' There was a sudden urgency about his voice. 'Now you're here I want to ask you a favour.' The faintest movement of his head in the direction of the drawing-room needed no interpretation. He didn't want his mother to hear. 'I'll wait for you in the car.'

Five minutes later, Casey was being driven into a lay-by on the ring-road into Melchester.

'What is it, Michael?'

'I want you to ask someone to help on your decorations sub-committee.'

'Well . . . '

'I have no idea whether she'll be any use to you, but I can't think of any other way to get her to the ball.'

'Couldn't you just take her?' she probed gently.

'It's not that simple.'

'Oh, I see.' Casey grinned. 'Mother doesn't approve?'

'Mother doesn't know,' he said with uncharacteristic vigour. 'And she won't until it's too late to do anything about it. Jennie's a shorthand-typist at the office.'

'Oh, dear,' she said, hiding a smile at his mother's likely reaction.

He turned impulsively towards her.

'Oh, Casey. I didn't understand when you dumped me. I was so . . . angry. But now, well, it's suddenly very clear. When it's really love, you can't help yourself, can you?'

She laughed and laid her hand on his. 'No, Michael, you can't. And I'm truly glad you've found someone. Give me her telephone number. I find I have an urgent need for someone to keep notes for my sub-committee. And I'll be happy to invite you to sit at our table if you like. After all, I'll need an escort for Jennie.'

'Your husband won't object?'

'He's no reason to.'

'No,' he grinned. 'And I should know. Here. I've written it down for you.' He handed her a piece of paper then leaned across and kissed her cheek. 'You're a brick.'

'That's me. Miss Brick, the builder's daughter,' she laughed.

'Not any more, Casey. You're Mrs Brick, the builder's wife now.'

Her eyes dropped. 'Yes, of course.

How silly of me.'

'Yes, well. I'd better get you home. Before Mr Brick comes looking for you. You're staying in Ladysmith Terrace until the house is ready, aren't you?'

'Yes.' She swallowed hard. She wasn't about to explain that Annisgarth had been sold. She found she could even manage a little smile. The bush telegraph was alive and well in Melchester.

Gil was in the kitchen when she let herself in. He was banging some steak very hard and he didn't turn around when she came in.

'I've changed your tyre for you.' There was something ominous about his voice that threatened trouble and she viewed the stiff shoulders with misgiving.

'Thank you. I didn't have time.' She tried a little light banter. 'Mrs Hetherington summoned me to a meeting and I had to call a taxi. I was still late, though. Quite unforgivable. I distinctly saw her put a black mark against my name.'

'Really?' He swung around and faced her and with a shock she realised that he was really angry. 'You only had a lift one way, then?'

'I beg your pardon?'

'You might well do that, Casey Blake. You might well beg my pardon. How many other people do you suppose saw you cuddling up to your boyfriend in broad daylight on the ring-road?'

8

'Cuddling . . . ' She flinched as Gil cracked the steak another vicious blow with the mallet. Michael's chaste kiss on her cheek could hardly be described as cuddling. Then, as she realised what his anger meant, she let out a sudden peal of laughter. He was jealous. Furiously and gloriously jealous.

He turned and stared at her as if she had gone mad. 'What's so funny?' he demanded.

'Nothing,' she gasped finally, struggling for breath. 'I think you'd better pass me the mushrooms if you want them to survive.'

'Mushrooms?' he roared, grabbing her shoulders and shaking her. 'This is all I care for mushrooms!' His mouth crashed down upon hers and for a moment she was stunned into immobility. Then her lips parted and exultantly

215

she began to respond. Her bag fell to the floor as her arms found their way around his neck and her fingers entwined in the thick dark curls of his hair.

But he made no attempt to woo her, ignoring all the signals that she was his willing accomplice, his anger overriding all other emotions, until finally, unable to breathe, she was beating helplessly against his chest, desperate for air. He released her at last and as she staggered away she saw the triumph flashing in his dark eyes.

'You're mine, Casey. Bought and paid for. And no one else will have you. Do you hear me?' The vein at his temple was beating fiercely as he moved to take hold of her again, but she stepped back, chilled to the core by his rejection of her willing surrender and once more in icy control of herself.

'Ask me, Gil,' she demanded, her breast heaving beneath her sweater. 'Ask me. Very nicely.'

He stopped abruptly, his face dark

with the effort it took him to hold himself in check, his hands clenched into tight fists at his side. 'Damn you, Casey. I thought we had already agreed that you were to do the asking,' he grated.

'So had I,' Casey spat. 'I think perhaps you forgot, just for a moment.'

'Perhaps seeing you in Michael's arms drove it from my mind.' His eyes had gone to cold slates and she shivered.

'Did it, Gil?' She had intended to explain. But he had never thought it necessary to explain why he had walked into the lift at the Melchester Hotel with his arm around Darlene, telling her that it had been 'hell without her'. Well, to 'hell' with explaining. 'Perhaps you should have kept your eyes on the road,' she threw at him, her blue eyes flashing dangerously.

He lunged towards her, his hand biting into the soft flesh of her arm until she cried out, 'Gil! You're hurting me!' For a moment they hung there, in an angry mist. Then Gil shuddered and loosened his grip.

'Keep my eyes on the road?'

'Much safer. For everyone. Wouldn't you say?'

'Doubtless.' His voice was scathing. 'I'll try to remember that in future.' He turned back to the steak and viewed it with distaste. 'How do you want this?'

Casey breathed out very carefully as the crackling tension began to subside, gently rubbing some feeling back into her arm. She stared dully at the meat for a moment before looking at Gil. 'Rare, I think. Very rare,' she said, aware that her voice was not quite steady.

Gil's mouth cracked into an ironic smile. 'Bloody? But definitely unbowed.'

'Pass me the mushrooms, Gil,' she said. 'It's been a long day and I'm tired.'

* * *

'How's the house coming on?' Gil finally raised his head from the letter that had, until now, claimed any attention he had to spare from his breakfast.

Casey, equally riveted by a long letter from her mother, looked up. 'What? Oh, I've picked out some wallpaper for the bedroom, but I don't know when I'll be able to start. I've taken on a couple more commissions this week,' she said, absently. 'Mum and Dad seem to be having a whale of a time. Dad is much better.'

'That, at least, is good news. But I didn't mean this house, Casey. I can see exactly what you're doing to this house. More important, I'm having to *live* with what you're doing to this house. Please, couldn't you just leave the bedroom as it is for the moment?'

She looked up from her letter. 'If you like.'

'I do like,' he said, with some feeling. 'But I was talking about Annisgarth. How long before it's finished.'

'Annisgarth?'

Gil sighed. 'Could you give me your

undivided attention for a minute, do you think? Or is your mother such a compelling letter writer?'

Casey flushed. The first page was certainly more interesting than Gil might imagine and for the moment she wasn't quite sure how to handle what her mother had told her. She folded the letter away, leaving the rest to read later, and gave her full attention to Gil. 'Sorry. Annisgarth. A couple of weeks should do it. Why all the sudden interest?'

'There is nothing sudden about my interest in everything that concerns you, Casey.' His eyes were expressionless. 'And I do mean *everything*. You have been my total concern since the first time I kissed you.' He shook his head as if to clear it. 'I wanted to know when you would be finished because I think we should have a few days away somewhere.'

'A belated honeymoon?' Casey widened her eyes under expressive brows, taking care to hide the sudden rise in her heartbeat. 'Has business picked up so much that you can afford to spare the time?'

'Sarcasm really doesn't suit you, Casey.' Gil put down his letter and looked steadily across the table at her. 'I've completed the arrangements for the future management of O'Connor Construction. It was never my intention to run it personally. Our marriage, however, is another matter. I think it's time both of us gave a little thought as to whether there is any point in continuing with the arangement.'

Casey felt the colour drain from her cheeks in a sudden rush. 'The house will be finished in a couple of weeks. But then there's the ball. Can you . . . ' she found a need to clear her throat ' . . . can you wait that long?'

'It seems I must,' he replied, without visible emotion, and yet Casey was certain that the tension in his face had increased if anything. 'But no longer, I think. Every man has his breaking-point and I seem to have somewhat overestimated my capacity for endurance.'

'Endurance, Gil?' she asked softly.

'I'm sure I don't have to explain what it's like to lie alongside you night after night, waiting for you to come to your senses.'

Casey quickly stifled the surge of compassion that rose in her throat. 'You could ask — '

'Very nicely. I know,' he interrupted grimly. 'No, thank you.' He paused as if half expecting something else from her. Then he shrugged. 'After this wretched ball, then.'

'Yes. I've taken on other work. But nothing that won't wait for a week.' She waited, hoping that he would soften, give her an opening to squeeze through, but he just nodded.

She allowed her eyes to linger on his bent head as he gave his full attention to the remainder of his post. He looked gaunt and tired and her mirror told her that she looked little better. Gil was right. It was time to settle things between them.

She had had enough of long nights, unable to sleep for the closeness of his body. Longing to reach out and touch him but unable to find the right moment, the right words. If only he had spoken one loving word she would have been unable to help herself. He wasn't the only one being tested to the edge of endurance.

Instead he had insisted that she was his property; that he had bought her along with the business, and hurt pride demanded that he should make the first move, offer some token of his need for her.

But she was afraid, very afraid that unless she goaded him beyond control he would never make it. And she knew too, in some deep part of her mind, that if she goaded him into taking her he would never forgive himself.

Life was short, and Gil Blake was the man who filled her dreams. And maybe it was a little greedy to expect him to tell her that he loved her. After all, he had never told her he loved her when they first met, and she had been more than willing then to take him as a lover. Maybe her love would be enough for both of them.

But it would be a month before they could get away, and the thought of another month spent like the last was unbearable. After the row when he had seen Michael kissing her, Gil had withdrawn into a shell. He no longer probed her for weakness, or teased her or laughed when they were alone. In public he still portrayed the devoted husband, but in private there was nothing but intense and painful politeness.

She touched the perfect red rose on the breakfast table testifying that yet another week had passed since their wedding. But since that first Saturday, when he had brought it up and eaten breakfast sitting on the edge of their bed, it had been more an exclamation mark than a token of love. A reminder that they were living with an unexploded bomb ticking away. And both of them were perfectly aware that they had to tiptoe around it, because one clumsy move could blow their lives apart.

He looked up and caught her staring at him. 'What are you thinking about?' he asked, suddenly intent.

Her lips curved into a soft smile. 'Nothing. Nothing at all.'

His eyes narrowed. 'Really?' When she didn't answer he stood up and glanced at his watch. 'Aren't you going to be late for Brownies?'

'Brownies?' She started from her reverie and leapt to her feet. 'Oh, lord! We're meeting here today. I'm sorry, I should have warned you, but . . . well, you usually go out straight after breakfast. I didn't think you'd be around to be bothered by them.'

'Who said I'd be bothered?' he challenged, suddenly angry. 'Or perhaps you would prefer me out of the way?'

Casey shook her head, surprised by

the vehemence of his reaction. 'Not unless you want to go. The girls are coming to see the kittens. I thought we could start them on their animal lover's badge.' She tried a small smile. 'And if I manage to find a home for any of them at the same time . . . '

'Oh, sneaky!' He unexpectedly returned her smile and she laughed.

'Absolutely. But I'll check with their mothers before I take any firm orders.'

Casey jumped at a sharp rap on the doorknocker. 'That'll be Matty.'

'You'd better go and let her in.'

She hesitated, longing to just be able to throw her arms around him and kiss him. He gave her a little push in the direction of the door.

'Go on. She'll think you're not in.' A second rap echoed his words and reluctantly she left him, aware that he was staring after her with a bitter little smile creasing the corners of his mouth.

'I'm not too early, am I?' Matty asked breathlessly, dumping a bag in the nearest chair. 'To be honest, I thought I was on the late side and I've been rushing.'

'You're fine. It'll be fifteen minutes before the girls start arriving.'

'Hello, Matty,' Gil greeted her warmly. 'There's some coffee left. Would you like a cup?'

Matty raised an eyebrow at Casey. 'He's not suggesting he made it, is he?'

'Heaven forbid!' Casey said, with rather more feeling than she had intended and caught a slight raising of Matty's eyebrows.

'I'd love one if it's no bother, Gil.'

'Nothing is too much trouble for you, Matty,' Gil replied easily.

Matty laughed. 'Save your smooth chatter for the typists in your office, Gil. They're young enough and perhaps they're silly enough to believe it.'

'Oh, they do,' he said. 'They are.' He threw a telling glance at Casey. 'And Casey can pour one out for me while she's fetching yours.'

Matty, still laughing, shook her head and followed Casey through to the kitchen. 'He doesn't fool me,' she said. 'Gil's a one-woman man if ever I saw one.'

'Is there such an animal?'

'Far and few, my dear. But yes, they do exist.' She looked up sharply. 'Surely you don't doubt it?'

'Oh, no. Of course not.' And when Gil appeared in the doorway to claim his coffee she tried very hard to put some genuine warmth into her smile. Matty was nobody's fool.

He flickered a surprised glance in her direction as he took the cup. 'Thanks, darling,' he said, casually, then grinned wickedly. 'And when you're making your little monsters cocoa and biscuits, you won't forget me, will you?'

'Cocoa and biscuits!' Casey exclaimed.

'Oh, they'll love you,' Matty said, laughing.

Gil's eyes meshed with Casey's. 'I rather think I should like that.' Before she could think of a suitable reply a knock at the door heralded the arrival of the girls. They quickly took over the house, settling in small groups to write about their own pets before going into the scullery in excited pairs to meet Cat and her kittens.

Gil produced some Polaroid film and totally won the girls' hearts by taking endless photographs of them with the kittens, and they wrung from him a promise that they could come back and see them again whenever they liked.

Casey sighed as the last of the girls whispered a shy little, 'Goodbye, Mr Blake. Thank you, Mr Blake.'

'You'll regret that,' Casey warned him, as she shut the door.

Gil shook his head. 'No, I won't. I loved every minute of it.' And it was true, she thought. He had treated the girls with a grave and patient courtesy and they had responded with total adoration. He would make any little girl a perfect father. 'Anyway, you'll be the one they bother. You're here more than me.'

Casey allowed herself to laugh. 'If you think that, Gil Blake, you know nothing about little girls. They'll lie in wait for you.'

'Well, that'll make a pleasant change, won't it?'

They stood awkwardly for a moment. 'Aren't you working today?' Casey asked finally.

'No, I'm not working. I thought I'd spend a quiet day at home with my wife, if it isn't too inconvenient. Or am I interfering with your plans for the day? What were they, Casey? A quiet little lunch somewhere with Michael, followed by an afternoon in bed — '

Her hand connected with his face with a crack that seemed to echo around the room. She stood rigid as the bright handprint appeared on his cheek where she had hit him, angrily ignoring the tears that threatened to overwhelm her.

'Did that make you feel better?' Gil's grey eyes glittered as he challenged her.

'Yes!' She swung again, but this time he was ready for her, his hand catching her arm mid-swing and holding it there.

Furiously she lifted her other arm, but he caught it easily with his free hand, holding her at bay as she struggled against his grip.

'No, Casey,' he said, with ominous calm. 'I don't think so. Once was quite enough.' He jerked her close against his chest, his mouth inches from her own. 'Now it's my turn.'

His mouth was hard and demanding and a great shuddering sigh shook her as she fell against him, her hands reaching for him, her fingers entwining themselves in his hair, pulling him down, her lips parting to his urgent probing tongue. They crashed together to the floor, sending the coffee-table and its lamp tumbling over as they tore at their clothes, her navy sweatshirt disappearing to the other side of the room, his shirt buttons flying as her fingers trembled with her need to touch him, hold him, feel his warm skin against her.

'Casey . . . ' he groaned.

'Don't speak . . . ' Then she groaned

in turn as he brushed his fingers against the hardened tip of her breast. His mouth breathed a trail of kisses down her throat to replace his caressing fingers, suckling fiercely, making her gasp with the fierce longing that stabbed through her. She kicked to free her legs from her tracksuit trousers. Gil paused in his attentions to her breast and stripped away the remainder of her clothes, his eyes lingering as his hand stroked her thigh and her legs parted involuntarily to invite his touch.

Gil shed the remainder of his clothes without ceremony and for a brief moment she was able to glory in the sight of his vigorous, deeply tanned body. Then he was on her, pinning her to the floor and escape was no longer an option, even if she had wanted it.

But escape was the furthest thing from her mind; she was exactly where she wanted to be, with Gil, his body hard and pulsating as he moved against her, his voice grating the longed-for love words in her ear, a warm ache filling her lower body as she arched upwards to meet him.

She pushed feverishly against him, parting her thighs as the ache became almost a pain in her increasing need for him. When she thought she could stand it no longer he came into her and she cried out with the fierce pleasure-pain as the soft flesh parted.

For a shocked moment Gil hesitated, poised above her, and she saw the wonder in his eyes, then with a fierce throaty cry he drove on, stoking the fire of passion he had lit within her until she was consumed in its flames, burning up as desire exploded into wave after wave of pleasure. Then Gil groaned savagely as she felt his own exultant release, before lowering himself gently against her.

For a brief perfect moment he lay there, his head on her breast, then with a deep shuddering sigh he rolled over and sat up.

'I'm sorry, Casey.' He raked long fingers through his hair. 'You should have told me.'

'That I was a virgin?' Without his body to cover her she suddenly felt very naked. She sat up and drew her knees up to her chin. 'I rather assumed you would find out for yourself.' She tried a smile. 'Sooner or later.'

His eyes gleamed as he took her hand and gently kissed the fingertips. 'Later, rather than sooner, I think.'

'Does it matter now?'

He raised his eyes from contemplation of her hand. 'I would have been . . . gentler.'

A delightful blush coloured her cheeks. 'You could be gentler . . . now.'

He pushed the damp strands of hair back from her face and pressed his lips against her forehead. 'It doesn't hurt?'

'No. Except, my back . . . ' His face creased in concern as she turned to see what she had done. 'I was lying on a half-eaten biscuit.'

Gil gave a sudden hoot of laughter. 'In that case, my darling, we'd better try and make it to the bedroom before we make love again.' Without waiting for her approval he scooped her up into his arms, carried her up the stairs and deposited her on the bed. 'Now, we'll do it the slow way,' he murmured, as he joined her, and lay propped up on one elbow, tracing with the lightest fingertip the contour of her breast. 'Since you asked so nicely.'

She refused to rise to his teasing. Instead she stretched out her arms to him. 'Do you want me to say please?'

'Only if you want to, Mrs Blake,' he replied, his eyes black with desire.

'Please, Gil, make love to me — ' His mouth claimed hers before she could finish, his probing tongue rekindling the flames of passion, his long sensitive fingers stoking up the fires that had been damped down for far too long.

Tentatively she reached out to trace her own pattern of exploration down his throat and across his chest. She revelled in the feel of his muscles contracting under the touch of her fingers. Shyly she touched his skin with the tip of her tongue and when he groaned looked up, startled.

'Don't stop,' he begged, and with growing confidence she smiled.

'Do you like that?' she asked.

'Witch! You know I do!'

'And this?' She slid her hand across his hard flat stomach.

'Go on,' he gasped as she hesitated.

Exultant at the effect she was having on him, she threw the last shreds of reserve to the four winds and allowed her hand to reach out and feel his hard need of her. At her touch he lost all semblance of self-control. He threw her on to her back and positioned himself above thighs already wide to receive him. With a fierce cry of pleasure he buried himself deep within her, holding himself still for a long moment, until she pushed against him, and her answering cry, 'Please, Gil!' drove them both over the edge of ecstasy and they fell asleep tangled in each other's arms.

Casey woke to find Gil staring at her.

'Hello, Mrs Blake. How do you feel?'

She allowed a slow smile of satisfaction to creep across her face. 'Married.'

'I should think you do.' A small crease worried his forehead. 'And do you think you'll like being a 'proper' wife?'

'From what I've experienced so far, I'd say it beats being an 'improper' one hands down.'

He grinned lopsidedly down at her. 'Yes. I had the feeling you were enjoying yourself.'

'And you? Were you enjoying yourself, Gil?'

'I hardly thought you needed to ask. But yes.' His grey eyes twinkled. 'I think you could say that I enjoyed myself quite thoroughly.' He sat up and she gave a moan as he moved away from her. He dropped a kiss on her mouth. 'You mustn't be greedy, sweetheart. I'm going to run you a bath.'

Casey stretched languidly. 'That sounds lovely. And I'm starving.'

'Well, yes. It is three o'clock in the

afternoon. We seem to have missed lunch.'

Half an hour later Casey pushed away her plate and sat back. 'You make a wonderful omelette, Gil.' She propped her head on her hands and looked across at him. 'You're pretty good at everything.'

'Am I?' He grimaced. 'I made a fair old mess of our marriage. I had actually got to the point where I thought I would have to let you go.'

Casey paled. 'Go?'

He nodded. 'You were so unhappy, it was making my heart break. I had thought that keeping you and Michael apart would be some sort of repayment for the way you treated me all those years ago.'

'No, Gil . . .'

He seemed not to hear. 'Silly. I discovered that I loved you too much. When I saw him kissing you I knew I'd have to let you go to him if you wanted to. No point in us both being miserable.'

She hugged the knowledge that he loved her deep inside her, keeping it to take out and cherish when she had some time to enjoy it. Now she had something far more important to do. 'Gil, listen to me.' He looked up at the urgency in her voice. 'I telexed Mum on the boat.'

His brows shot up. 'Whatever for?'

'That letter. The one sacking you. As soon as I saw it I knew it wasn't from Dad.' He tried to interrupt but she shook her head impatiently. 'Dad had no formal education. He never wrote a letter when a phone call or a meeting would do.'

'I don't understand, Casey. What are you saying?'

'My father would have stood in front of you and told you exactly what he thought of you. And I doubt very much if he would have sacked you. Far more likely to have demanded that you marry me.' She thought about it. 'If I had run to him it would have saved a lot of misery.' She shook her head. The misery was over. 'My mother knew that, which was presumably why she never asked him to deal with you. You see, when she witnessed my precipitate flight from the woods she had the wit to wait to see who followed me. Then she typed that very polite letter of dismissal. I recognised the typeface of her portable. The cheque was presumably to cover her conscience.'

Gil shook his head. 'But there was my P45, and the letter was at the site office, waiting for me.'

'A very resourceful woman, my mother. She had the office keys. But you don't have to take my word for it. That's what her letter was about. Her confession.' She fetched the letter from the mantelpiece and handed it to him. 'Read it for yourself.'

He took the letter, but made no move to read it. 'But why, Casey?'

Casey sighed. 'Mum came from a 'county' family, Gil. Pony Club, Cheltenham Ladies' College, all that. Then she met Dad. Her family disapproved.' She laughed. 'They could hardly do anything else, could they? All he had to commend him was a broad back, a smile that could charm birds down from the trees — their pheasants in all probability — and an eye for business. So she ran away with him.'

Gil's eyes narrowed. 'Are you telling me that she regretted it?'

'No. Not that. She loves Dad as much now as she did then, I think. But it didn't stop her knowing how much she had lost.'

'And you weren't to be allowed to make the same sacrifice?'

Casey stood up. 'Read her letter, Gil. It's an odd mixture. Half apology, half justification. After all, you wouldn't have gone to Australia and made the cash to rescue us all if she hadn't chased you off.' She brushed back a tear threatening to spill down her cheek.

Gil reached out and picked up the letter.

Casey fed the cat then went to wash

up. The house settled down silently, as if waiting while Gil slowly turned the pages of her mother's letter. She made the tea and poured two cups and placed them on the table then sat down opposite him, a sudden qualm of misgiving at his still and silent withdrawal into the close-written pages.

Finally he looked up. Casey felt the shock of his eyes jolt through her. The tenderness had gone. Instead her husband, this man who had just made love to her as though the world were about to end, was regarding her with utter and complete distaste.

'Very interesting, Casey. You and your father have my most sincere apologies for misjudging you, at least for the past. What a pity that you forgot to tell me not to read the rest of the letter.'

Bewildered, Casey looked from Gil to the letter and then back again. 'I don't know what you're talking about.'

'No?'

'Gil. Please. I only read the first couple of pages. What did she say to make you so angry?'

His mouth twisted into a mockery of a smile. 'I don't blame you for trying, Casey. And I have to admit that you had me fooled.' A vein beat fiercely at his temple. 'I really played into your hands too, didn't I? Admitting how much I wanted you?'

'Gil! This is crazy!'

'Is it?' He stood up, filling the kitchen. 'It didn't take much to stage that little scene, did it, Casey? I was primed, ready to go off the minute you touched me. And you didn't waste any time. One word from your mother that Gil Blake was in the money and you opened your legs fast enough!'

9

'That's enough!' Casey's shocked voice cut sharply across Gil's harsh tone.

'What's the matter, sweetheart? The plain, honest truth a bit much for you?' He angrily brushed aside her attempt to deny whatever it was he was accusing her of. 'I cared for you, Casey. Really cared. You seemed so vulnerable, so innocent. And I was actually fool enough to think that you returned my feelings. Laughable, really. Because you went to great lengths to make it quite clear that I was just someone to have fun with until a 'suitable' husband came along, poor sap.'

'No, Gil . . . '

'Oh, yes, Gil,' he mocked. 'And I lost my head completely. I wasn't good enough to marry you, but I was sure as hell going to give you something to remember!' He laughed shortly. 'Bad joke. You certainly knew how to put a stop to that.'

Casey's eyes were filling with tears. She didn't know what she was crying for. Only that everything she had ever wanted was crumbling away before her. 'It wasn't like that,' she protested, but he was beyond hearing.

'For years there was nothing else to drive me on but the need to wipe out the memory of the way you humiliated me. It was that image of you that drove me on until I could afford to buy you. Not that I expected you to love me.' He shook his head. 'Love was no longer part of the equation. But it didn't take a genius to know that money would be enough . . . '

She turned to run then, but he caught her wrist and turned her roughly to face him. 'And I found that I was very good at making money, because I wasn't afraid of taking risks. I'm just like your father, Casey. Except I took bigger risks because I had nothing to lose.'

Casey stood riveted, stunned by the bitter outpouring of Gil's soul. A shuddering sigh escaped from her lips, nothing more.

He released her wrist and turned away from her then, his shoulders slumped. 'But the joke was on me, Casey. The day we married I discovered that owning your body was never going to be enough, not if your heart was absent. I found I had to have all of you.' He ran long fingers distractedly through his hair. 'And for a while I thought it was going to happen. Not immediately. But I was prepared to wait.' He straightened. 'But you haven't got a heart, have you, Casey? Just a little bank vault that only opens for deposits?'

Confused and numb with shock, unable to understand or feel anything, although she knew the pain would come, she stared blankly at his rigid back. 'I'll move my things up to the attic,' she said, without expression.

He swung round, his eyes ablaze in

his white face. 'Oh, no, Casey! You won't be moving your things anywhere. I've been celibate on your behalf for quite long enough.' He looked at his watch and swore under his breath. 'We'll have to continue this absorbing conversation another time. I forgot to tell you . . . ' his eyes flickered towards her ' . . . what with one thing and another . . . that we're taking Darlene and her husband out to dinner tonight at the Club. I said we'd pick them up at seven-thirty.'

Casey snapped out of the state of mental paralysis that was threatening to overwhelm her. 'Her husband?'

'He arrived from Sydney a couple of days ago.'

Casey had assumed that Mrs Forster was divorced, not that it mattered any more. 'You expect me to go out with you and be sociable this evening as if nothing has happened?' She heard her voice rising hysterically.

'Why not? For an actress of your skill it shouldn't hold any difficulties. And when you marry for money, entertaining goes with the territory. Entertaining in every sense of the word.'

'I didn't marry you for your money!'

'That's not what you said when we had lunch at the Watermill.'

The colour drained from her face as she recalled the conversation. 'I didn't mean it, Gil.'

'Not then perhaps. But just then you didn't think I had enough money to do much more than save your skin. You've apparently had second thoughts since you had that letter from your mother.'

'It isn't true!'

'No? In that case why aren't you planning your wedding to Michael Hetherington right now? He was pressing you hard enough in the dining-room of the Bell a few weeks back.'

Angry patches of colour darkened her cheeks. 'You were spying on me before we were married!'

'No. Pure chance, I assure you. Those little booths are so discreet. But it did rather force my hand, and messing up the wedding of the year did add a little extra dimension to the revenge I had planned. The finishing touch if you like.'

'Tell me, Gil,' she rasped, 'what would you have done if I'd already been married?'

'Ruined your father, and afterwards I would have let you know why,' he said, without hesitation.

She was too shocked to reply. Apparently satisfied with the impression he had made, he eyed her coldly. 'Now, if you'll excuse me, I'll go and collect the Jaguar. At least I won't have to drive that damned pram on wheels of yours ever again!'

He strode towards her and Casey shrank back, wanting to run, as hard and fast as she could. But even if there had been anywhere to run to her legs had turned to putty and she made no effort at resistance as his mouth staked his claim to her with as much tenderness as a goldrush miner driving his mark into the hard ground.

'Gil!' Her voice was shrill and he turned in the doorway. She paused, trying to regain control of her voice and of herself.

'Yes?' he asked impatiently, and something inside her snapped.

'If you're so damned rich, what are we doing living in a house that didn't even have a bathroom . . . ?'

His smile didn't reach his eyes. 'Put it down to a whim. I thought you deserved a taste of how the other half lives.'

He closed the door carefully, leaving her standing, bewildered, hurt, angry, in the centre of the little world she had begun to think of as her home.

Reluctantly she returned to the kitchen and stared down at her mother's letter. Almost dreading to read it, she reached out and took it from the table. She hadn't got past her mother's confession about Gil when she read it over the breakfast table but now, if she was to find out what had provoked Gil's angry outburst, she must read it all.

She skipped quickly through the first two pages, and found that once her mother had cleared up the mystery of Gil's dismissal she had launched into a chatty report of life aboard ship.

As she read her mother's account about a conversation with some Australians she had met on board ship, she felt her blood run cold. They had been very impressed that Mr and Mrs O'Connor had been lucky enough to capture so rich a prize as Gil Blake for a son-in-law. In fact, she told Casey indignantly, she was sure they hadn't believed her until she had shown them the cutting from the *Melchester Post* with the photograph of the wedding that someone had sent her.

Darling, you must have known how unhappy I was that you decided to marry Gil Blake in such haste, but I realise now that I should have trusted your judgement.

No one was happier than me to see

Daddy retire after that nasty turn he had, but I had the feeling that Gil was hard pushed to find the money. How wrong can you be? Dolly told me that everyone in Australia knows how he staked a friend to go drill for oil in some place ... I can't remember where ... and he apparently found it. Now they're both millionaires several times over.

Clever girl. In retrospect it is so obvious that you would never have let Michael go unless you had something better ...

The letter fluttered from her lifeless fingers and a low shuddering sob shook her as she collapsed in a heap on the kitchen floor.

A long bath and the careful application of makeup covered the worst ravages of her stormy outbreak of tears. She heard Gil come in when she was dressing and held her breath as he bounded up the stairs. To her relief he went straight into the bathroom, and she hurried to put the finishing touches to her hair so that she could be dressed before he appeared. But her fingers betrayed her, slipping and fumbling as she twisted her hair into a severe chignon and she was still tugging at the zip of her black chiffon gown when the door opened and Gil, a towel wrapped around his waist, stepped towards her, making the room seem altogether too small. She lost control of her fingers and let her hand fall lifelessly to her side.

'You don't have to struggle, Casey. It's a husband's duty — a husband's *pleasure* — to help his wife with her zip.' He turned her round and stood behind her, regarding her steadily through the dressing-table mirror. 'Of course, it's a greater pleasure to take it down.' His hand hesitated for a second, then he shrugged and pulled it firmly up and fastened the hook at the neck. 'Shame we haven't the time right now.' Casey's cheeks coloured with a fiery blush and she turned away from his mocking gaze and turned to leave the room. 'Sit down, Casey. Keep me company while I dress.'

Casey subsided obediently on to the dressing-table stool and carefully regarded her nails while Gil moved about the room.

'It's all right, it's safe to look up now. I've got my trousers on.' Her head jerked up and she glared at him. 'But I need a hand with my tie. And I'm sure you know how to tie a bow-tie.' He held out the scrap of black silk and reluctantly she rose to her feet and took it from him.

A smile played about his lips as she was forced to stand on tiptoe and put her arms around his neck to settle the tie into place. As she struggled to keep her balance he placed his hands around her waist and steadied her. She instantly stopped.

'Go on!' he insisted, and despite her shaking hands it was finally done and for the moment there was a blessed release from the touch that she most yearned for, and which could never again bring her the joy she had experienced that afternoon.

He leaned forward and examined the result in the mirror. 'There. I knew you would be able to do it. That's one of the joys of a well brought up wife. She has all the social graces. That deserves a reward.'

'Stop it, Gil!'

Gil ignored her plea and opened his wardrobe. When he turned back he was holding a small velvet box. He opened it and lifted out a pair of earrings, diamond drops to complement the ring glittering on her left hand.

'No. I won't take them.'

The smile never left his mouth, but his eyes glittered coldly. 'Don't be silly. Darlene made a special trip to London to choose them for you.' He placed them in her hand. 'She'll expect you to be wearing them tonight.'

'Well, now, it wouldn't do to offend Darlene, would it? Perfect, efficient, beautiful and conveniently married

Darlene.' Casey found that even when you were breaking in half a sort of conversation was possible. She regarded her reflection in the mirror. 'She has excellent taste.'

'She's an excellent woman, and her husband is a lucky man, as he well knows.'

'And does he know about your assignations with his wife at the Melchester Hotel?' The words were out before she could recall them.

'Assignations?' There was an ominous quiet about the word that appalled Casey, but she had gone too far to draw back.

'I saw you,' she whispered. 'You had your arm around her as you got into the lift. You said it had been 'hell' without her.'

Gil stared at her with a strange expression lighting his eyes. 'And what were you doing in the Melchester Hotel on a Monday morning?'

He didn't deny it, knew exactly what she was talking about. 'I was taking a room. I thought I'd treat myself to a bath.'

'And did you enjoy it?'

She shook her head. 'I didn't . . . stay . . . '

He remained silent and she looked up, surprising for a moment an expression that she couldn't decipher, before his face closed.

'We'd better go.' He shrugged into his dinner-jacket and minutes later they were purring along the ring-road that led to the new housing estates on the far side of the town.

Darlene and her husband were waiting for them. She smiled warmly at Casey. 'I'm glad to meet you at last, Casey. Gil's told me so much about you. This is my husband Peter.'

Peter, a slim fair man, who towered above the small dark figure of his wife, grinned and shook hands with her. 'Hello, Casey. Shall we have a drink here before we go?'

'Better not,' Gil said. 'We're running a bit late. How's this place?'

'It'll do for now,' Peter replied

257

amiably. 'But Darlene has her heart set on a real English cottage — '

'We've seen a couple of promising houses already,' Darlene interrupted.

'You're house hunting so soon after moving in?' Casey asked.

'This is just rented. Gil put me up in the Melchester after he sent a frantic plea for me to come on ahead of Pete. But I can't stand living out of a suitcase. Now he's arrived we can look for somewhere permanent.'

'Oh, I see,' she said, and caught Gil looking at her with amusement, understanding that she didn't see at all.

'Peter is going to put O'Connor Construction on the right tracks for me,' he offered by way of enlightenment as he handed her into the car.

'You're a builder, Peter?' she asked, over her shoulder.

'An accountant,' he replied, grinning as he saw her shocked expression. 'But O'Connor's is safe enough. Gil's already warned me off selling the family silver.'

She glanced at Gil's stiff profile as he drove through the great wrought-iron gates of the Club and pulled up at the main entrance to drop them before driving away to find a parking place. 'Some of the people there worked for my father for a very long time,' she said to Peter.

'Gil said it was important to you.'

'I see he couldn't wait to give you your earrings,' Darlene laughed, as they handed their wraps to the cloakroom attendant.

Casey touched them self-consciously. 'I understand I have you to thank for the choice.'

'Me?' She shook her head. 'I picked them up when I drove down to fetch Peter from the airport, but Gil ordered them when he had to go to London a couple of weeks ago.'

'A couple of weeks ago?'

'Yes. Gil really chewed me out for breaking up your weekend, but when the stock market started to go haywire I knew I had to call him. That's why he wanted me here, after all, to keep him in touch . . . '

Casey felt herself go cold. 'The stock market? On a Sunday?'

Darlene looked at her in surprise. 'It was Monday in Oz,' she said gently.

'Monday?' Casey tried to pull her wits together. She was beginning to sound half-witted, repeating everything that Darlene said. 'Oh. Of course . . . I never thought.'

She made it through the dinner somehow, and if Darlene and Peter thought that their hosts were a little distracted they were too wrapped up in each other to let it bother them. Casey watched them dancing, holding each other close.

'We could try that if you like,' Gil suggested, breaking into her thoughts.

'Of course.' She was his wife, bought and paid for, and now she understood that she would do her best to give good value for money.

Gil danced with an easy grace, his arm draped lightly around her waist, holding her firmly pressed against him. In another time, another place, it would have been heaven. Now the touch of his hand and his body, his thighs against hers as they moved together, were only a torment.

'Enjoying yourself, darling?' he breathed in her ear.

She had been smiling so hard all evening that it felt as though her lips were fixed in a permanent grimace. 'It's absolutely perfect,' she breathed between clenched teeth. 'Darling.' She tipped her head back and flickered a look at him from under long dark lashes. 'And I never thanked you properly for my lovely earrings.'

He grinned down at her. 'You can do that later.'

She took a breath, reinforced her smile and murmured, 'I can't wait.' He stumbled and roughly suggested they sit down.

Casey's eyes narrowed as he stopped a waiter and ordered a brandy. He saw her look and raised his glass. 'To soft beds and hard battles,' he toasted her, and tipped the liquid down his throat.

Darlene and Peter rejoined them, but only to excuse themselves. 'Peter's still a bit jet-lagged,' Darlene apologised. 'I've called a taxi.'

'Oh, but we would have taken you home,' Casey protested.

'No. You stay and enjoy yourselves. Thanks for a lovely evening.'

'I'll telephone you in the week,' Casey promised. 'We could have lunch, and I'll introduce you to Charlotte. If there's a country cottage going she'll know about it.'

'Jet-lagged my aunt Fanny,' Gil muttered, as they disappeared through the door. 'They can't wait to get into bed together.'

Casey looked up sharply, suddenly realising that her husband had had altogether more alcohol than was good for him. 'I think we'll follow their example,' she said firmly, and stood up.

He stood up and regarded her with

irony. 'Oh, Casey. Can this possibly be true?'

In reply she slipped her arm around his waist and slid her hand into his trouser pocket. His eyes widened in shock as she felt for the car keys and extracted them before he realised what she was doing. 'Casey!' He lurched towards her.

She dangled the keys before him. 'Come on, Gil. I consider it my wifely duty to get you out of here before you make a complete and utter fool of yourself.'

She found the car and Gil subsided, unprotesting, into the passenger-seat. Casey examined the controls nervously, refusing to ask for assistance. Once she was sure which was the reverse gear she backed out with extreme care, aware that her foot was trembling on the clutch.

She drove slowly down the driveway and pulled out into the quiet road. Pleased with herself, she moved up through the gears, enjoying the feel of the car and gaining confidence as the controls became more familiar.

'We could go a little faster, Casey,' Gil broke in once they were on the ring-road. 'I've seen you driving your little van at twice this speed along here.'

'Do you spend your entire life spying on me?' Casey demanded. When he didn't answer she stamped her foot down on the accelerator and Gil swore as the car shot forward, throwing them both back hard in their seats.

'Dear heaven! I take it all back. You were doing fine!' But Casey ignored him, only slowing when they reached their turn-off. She parked neatly in front of her van and climbed out.

Gil opened the front door and turned on the light. 'I think I could do with another drink,' he said. 'That was a very sobering experience.'

'No.'

He turned in the act of pouring a brandy and regarded Casey's over-bright eyes and hectic cheeks. 'No?'

'I prefer not to think that you have to

be drunk to make love to me.'

She tried to blot out the memory of their lovemaking that afternoon. She responded to his touch, she couldn't help herself, and cried out as he brought her once more to perfect release. But afterwards, when he rolled over and turned his back on her, she let the tears fall, taking care not to let her silent weeping disturb his sleep.

* * *

'Are you all right, Casey?' Jennie asked tentatively. 'You look very pale.'

Casey hid her irritation with the girl. There was no excuse for her edginess. She had been glad enough to help Michael along with his secret romance, and, although Jennie had been a trifle self-conscious with her at first, once she realised that Casey was no threat she had been an enormous help.

She eased her fingers across her forehead. If only her headache would clear she could cope. Feeling guilty, she made herself smile.

'I'm fine, Jennie, really. How are the florists getting on with the pillars in Reception?'

'Nearly done. It looks beautiful. I don't think I've ever seen so many flowers at one time.'

'Yes, there are rather a lot. Frankly the theme 'moonlight and roses' was a bit over the top for my taste, but it does look pretty.' Her heart sank as she saw Mrs Hetherington bearing down upon her.

'You seem to be on schedule, Casey.' She glanced at Jennie. 'Who is this?'

'Jennie Stanford. She's been my right arm. I don't know what I would have done without her.'

Mrs Hetherington nodded graciously, already taking on her mantle as the evening's grand dame. 'Well, I hope you enjoy yourself tonight.'

'Michael has kindly volunteered to look after Jennie this evening,' Casey said quickly.

The older woman looked at the girl

more carefully, then, seeing nothing to disturb her in this slight figure, clad in dungarees and with her hair in a pigtail, smiled and sailed on.

Casey exchanged a look with the younger girl and they burst out laughing. 'Do be sure to enjoy yourself this evening, Jennie,' Casey mimicked, turning to pick up a box of pins.

'I intend to,' she replied, suddenly serious. 'I only plan to have one wedding night.'

Casey turned back to her in astonishment. 'Wedding night?' she breathed.

'Michael and I were married at the register office in Penborough this morning. That's where I live. Lived,' she corrected herself.

'Oh, my dear. My best wishes. But . . . ' She stopped. No point in spoiling her day by suggesting what Mrs Hetherington's reaction was likely to be. Besides, the manner of her marriage suggested that she already knew.

Jennie grinned. 'We'll be leaving the

ball a little early. Michael's taking me to France for our honeymoon.' She saw the doubt in Casey's face. 'We'll face the music when we get back.'

'I hope you'll both be very happy. And if I can do anything to help with the great escape, just ask.'

'It's all in hand. The fact that we've got a bedroom here to change this evening made everything simple.' She frowned. 'Look, why don't you go up and lie down for a while? There's not much left to do. I can easily finish this pinning.'

'Well . . . '

'Go on. I can cope.'

Casey managed a smile. 'Yes. I rather believe you can.'

'I'll bring you a cup of tea when I come up.'

Casey stretched out on the bed and tried to relax. At least here she was away from the constant strain of her relationship with Gil.

The nightmare of waking every morning, knowing that her marriage was a sham, an elaborate torture perpetrated on her by the man she loved to punish her for imagined crimes, was taking its toll. She was thinner than she had ever been, and a week earlier Charlotte had been moved to ask if she had seen a doctor.

There was no doctor on earth who had a cure for what ailed her. Only Gil could do that. But he had made it perfectly clear that she would remain his wife until he chose otherwise. And for the moment he chose that she should stay.

She had never again suggested she move up to the attic, or denied him his rights as a husband. Night after night he wrung from her the passionate response that their first coming together had promised, but without tenderness or warmth. And afterwards he turned wordlessly from her and fell into an exhausted sleep. She could only hope that eventually he would weary of this angry coupling and leave her alone to patch her life together.

She shifted restlessly on the bed, unable to settle. Finally, she rose and walked across to the window. Below, the workmen were placing lights all along the driveway. There were banks of flowers near the pool and small tables were being set out by an army of helpers drafted in for the occasion. It was a lovely evening, and she was sure that people would desert the ballroom in droves after dinner, to enjoy the cooler poolside seating.

The door opened behind her and she turned. Jennie carried in a tray of tea which she set down on the table. 'I thought you were going to lie down,' she admonished.

'I couldn't. I'm jumpy.'

'Relax. Everything's fine. Not a hiccup.'

'You've been marvellous. Especially with so much on your mind.'

'Being busy has helped.' She poured the tea. 'Come and sit down. You look worn to a shadow.'

'Be careful. Flattery like that could

go straight to my head.'

Jennie's hand flew to her mouth and Casey laughed at her stricken expression. 'Oh, lord. I shouldn't have said that. I'm sorry.'

'Don't be. I've just got a bit of a headache. A cup of tea will work wonders. How long have we got?'

Jennie consulted her watch. 'An hour. Mrs Hetherington issued strict instructions we were all to be in the ballroom by seven-thirty.'

'To receive her gracious thanks for all the hours of sweat we've put in to make her look good.'

Jennie grinned wickedly. 'Just think of her face tomorrow, when she reads Michael's note.'

'Jennie! She's your mother-in-law. I was always convinced that nobody deserved that fate, but I'm beginning to wonder if she deserves you!'

Jennie tried to look contrite, but failed. 'Is that why you decided not to marry Michael?' she asked with a giggle.

Casey's smiled faded. 'For a while I thought Michael and I would suit one another. But in the end I realised it wouldn't do. You can't marry without love.' And sometimes even that is not enough, she added silently.

Jennie won the toss to use the bathroom first and, by the time Casey had emerged, was wearing a simple long black dress that made her look a lot more dangerous than the dungarees she had worn earlier. 'You look lovely, dear,' Casey said and hugged her. A tap at the door proved to be Michael, and he whisked his 'date' away for a quiet walk in the gardens.

Casey took her time applying her make-up with the care needed to hide the dark shadows beneath her eyes. She was fastening the diamond drops into place when another tap made her twitch nervously. 'Come in.'

'Are you . . . ?' Gil stopped as Casey stood up and turned to face him.

'Quite ready,' she said in a cool dry voice that hardly seemed to belong to her these days. 'In fact I'm rather late. I'll be getting another black mark from Mrs Hetherington.' She picked up the tiny clutch-bag that matched the long deep blue taffeta ballgown she was wearing. It wasn't new. She hadn't the funds available herself to buy a new dress, but she had refused to give Gil the satisfaction of asking him for the money. 'Shall we go?'

'Not for a moment.' He stepped towards her and she felt herself vibrate with her need to put her arms around him and tell him how much she loved him. He slipped a long box from the pocket of his jacket. 'Sit down, Casey.'

She sank back on to the stool before the dressing-table and Gil fastened a diamond choker around her throat and then, his hands resting lightly on her bare shoulders, he regarded her steadily. Her reflection swam before her as she touched it. 'It's beautiful.'

'Yes, it's beautiful. You complement one another perfectly. Both of you are beautiful. And both of you are very expensive. The necklace I can afford — it only costs money. But I'm beginning to wonder if the cost of keeping you will be more than body and soul can bear.'

10

For a moment their eyes were locked through the looking-glass. 'You're breaking me into little pieces, Casey. I don't know how much longer I can go on with this charade.'

Casey could see the dark hollows at his temples and in his cheeks. It was plain that he was suffering just as much as she was and impulsively she turned and put her hand on his.

'Gil — ' There was a light tap at the door and it began to open. 'We can't talk now.'

'Casey?' It was Jennie. 'It's quarter to — Oh, I'm sorry, Mr Blake.'

His hands dropped from her shoulders. 'Gil, please. You must be Jennie.' He moved forward to shake hands. 'I'm sorry, I'm afraid I've been keeping Casey from her duties. We're just coming.'

The three of them walked down the staircase, where Casey carefully introduced Michael to Jennie, who thanked him so prettily for being her escort for the evening that Casey thought she might explode with repressed, if slightly hysterical laughter.

Michael turned to Gil and they eyed one another cautiously, in the manner of game cocks summing up the opposition, before shaking hands briefly. Then they all moved forward into the ballroom where they were joined by Charlotte and her boyfriend and Darlene and Peter.

Gil and Michael seemed to forget that they should dislike one another and the laughter from their table soon drew indulgent smiles from other, quieter parts of the room, and Gil hesitated only for a moment when Michael asked if Casey could be spared to dance with him.

'Congratulations, you naughty boy,' she said quietly, as he whisked her away across the dance-floor. 'When are you planning to escape?'

276

'Right now. Jennie's already gone out to the car, but I didn't want to leave without saying thank you. I'm just going up to get her things.' He looked serious. 'And I wanted to ask you one last favour.'

'Anything, Michael. Except tell your mother!'

'Not necessary. I've left a note where she'll find it tomorrow. But will you keep cave for me? I don't want to run into my mother while I'm carrying Jennie's suitcases down the stairs.'

'That would certainly take some explaining,' she laughed. 'We'll go as soon as the music stops.'

'Thanks, Casey.'

'It's my pleasure. And I hope you'll be very happy.' She hugged him impulsively.

The waltz came to halt and Casey glanced across to their table. Gil wasn't there, she noted with relief. It would have been rather tricky explaining that she was slipping away to assist in a secret runaway honeymoon, especially with four other people listening. She would tell him later.

She allowed Michael to lead her out into the hallway. It was quiet; those people not dancing had migrated out to the poolside bar. Giggling like naughty children, they ran quickly up the stairs. Casey unlocked the door and Michael followed her in.

'Those are the bags,' Casey said, indicating the two suitcases at the foot of the bed. Michael picked them up and turned.

'Oh! Gil,' he said, and grinned sheepishly. 'You've discovered our little secret.'

Gil stepped forward and hit Michael squarely on the jaw, and sent him sprawling across the floor.

Casey stared at her husband in horror, then fell to her knees and cradled Michael's head in her lap. 'Michael!' she cried. Then she glared up at Gil. 'Whatever do you think you've done?'

For a moment he stood bleakly

surveying the scene before him, ignoring the blood oozing from his knuckles.

'I'm sorry. I just saw red, I suppose. I had intended to be civilised.' He sank on to the end of the bed. 'It's not every day that your wife makes such elaborate plans to run away with her lover.'

Michael struggled to a sitting position while Casey ran to the bathroom for some water.

'You throw one hell of a punch, Blake,' Michael complained, wincing as Casey applied a cold wet towel to his face. 'I'm supposed to be driving to France tonight.'

'Casey can drive,' Gil said dully. 'But there's no need to go so far. Here.' He threw down a bunch of keys, and Casey felt the colour drain from her face as she saw the familiar tag.

'Annisgarth?'

'Yes. Annisgarth. You might as well have your house. I shan't have any use for it. I just hope to God you can be happy in it. One of us should have a chance to be happy, and whatever I do it's as sure as hell not going to be me,' he said bitterly.

Casey picked up the keys from the carpet. 'You bought Annisgarth for me?' she asked, her voice hardly more than a whisper. Her heart was pounding with a ridiculous sensation that might well have been happiness, but it was so long since she had felt the emotion that she couldn't be quite sure.

'Yes. And your father drove a hard bargain. Still, what the heck. It's only money, and lord knows I've more than enough of that.' He stood up. 'You needn't worry about anything. I'll organise a settlement for you, and Peter will look after the company. I've had enough of revenge.'

Michael cleared his throat and struggled to his feet, the towel still clutched to his chin. 'Might I have some say in this, do you think?'

Gil lifted his eyes and stared at him coldly. 'Is there something else? You've already got everything I ever wanted — isn't that enough?'

'An explanation would be — '

The door flew open and Jennie stood there, her arms akimbo on her hips. 'Michael Hetherington, if I have to wait one minute longer you'll be going on this honeymoon on your own,' she declared. Then she saw the cloth and the blood and with a little scream she flew across the room. Gil stared at them and then turned to Casey, totally bewildered.

'They were married this morning. It was supposed to be a secret.'

'Married?' he gasped. 'But they only just met!'

'Er — no. The introduction was for public consumption. For reasons that are none of our business, Michael and Jennie didn't want their relationship to become common knowledge.'

'But I saw you and . . . him . . . ' he indicated Michael with a flick of his hand ' . . . creeping up here like a pair of conspirators.'

'Michael was fetching Jennie's cases. I was supposed to be keeping watch.

Not a very good one, apparently.'

He ran his fingers wearily across his forehead. 'Oh, God. Oh, dear God. Michael . . . Whatever can I say?'

Michael grinned. 'You could congratulate me on my good fortune. And perhaps,' he suggested, 'you might offer your wife an apology?' His glance flickered curiously between them.

'You should offer to chauffeur them to France,' Casey said hotly. 'Or perhaps you still want me to do it?' she continued, with dangerous calm.

'I can manage,' Michael said quickly. 'And if we don't get going we'll miss the ferry.' He threw the towel to one side.

'I'll take your cases,' Gil offered. 'If anyone sees me, well, I'm sure I can make something up.'

'You usually do.' Casey's eyes kindled furiously.

Gil had the grace to look discomfited. 'Where's the car?'

Jennie told him, and a few minutes later they followed him down, Jennie leaning heavily on Casey's arm, a story about a sick headache and over-excitement already prepared if they should meet anyone interested enough to take any notice. They didn't.

Casey and Gil watched them drive away and then turned to each other. 'You could have broken his jaw,' she said reproachfully.

'I fully intended to.'

'Oh.' She looked down at her feet and then allowed a little smile to creep across her mouth. She peeped up at him from under her lashes. 'But then, honour satisfied, you were prepared to let me go away with him?'

He tucked his hand under her chin and lifted her face to his. 'I wanted you to be happy, Casey. I've hurt you so badly, and I thought if that was what you wanted I would have to let you go.'

'But preferably with Michael's jaw in two pieces?'

'Well, I'm only human.' He regarded her steadily, a question in his eyes.

'Human enough to kiss me?' she whispered.

'Oh, yes,' he said, and, gathering her in his arms, proceeded to demonstrate very thoroughly just how much he wanted to kiss her. How very human he could be.

When finally he raised his head, she smiled lazily. 'I don't think a car park is an appropriate place to complete this conversation.'

'I couldn't agree more, Mrs Blake.'

'It's rather rude to leave the party,' she reminded him.

'What party?'

He drove her slowly away from the town and up to Annisgarth. It sat in the not-quite-dark of midsummer, and the scent of roses hung in the air around them as they walked to the front door. Gil slid the key into the lock but Casey reached out and caught his arm.

'No. Not here.'

As he turned in question, he saw her staring down the hill to the darker shadow of the wood beneath them, and he smiled in understanding.

'I'll fetch a rug from the car.'

'We didn't have one before,' she reminded him.

'You were wearing jeans on that occasion. I think silk and diamonds merit a rug,' he said, and paused to kiss her.

'You could be right,' she agreed at last and reluctantly allowed him to fetch one.

When Gil rejoined her he had a rug over one arm, and the other he wrapped around her shoulders. 'Are you warm enough?'

'Yes. It's a beautiful night.'

'Perfect.'

He spread the rug and they lay down in the hollow, breathing in the scent of crushed germander. Gil reached for her then, but she stayed him. 'No, not yet. I have to tell you why I wanted to come here.'

His lips nuzzled her throat. 'I don't want to talk.'

'It's important, Gil. It was here it all

started to go so wrong.'

'Hush, Casey. It's all over.'

'No,' she insisted with absolute conviction. 'If we don't tell each other exactly how we feel, how we felt, it can all go wrong again.'

He allowed himself to plant the briefest kiss on her forehead and propped himself up on one elbow. 'I'll try to be patient. We've got all night.'

'I wanted you to know about the day I brought you here. Just before my eighteenth birthday.'

'I do remember,' he said, quietly.

'I wanted you to see the house because I thought . . . hoped . . . that you might like me enough to want to marry me, and I wanted you to know that it was possible.' He drew in a sharp breath, but she went on quickly. 'You hadn't said you loved me. But I thought perhaps you did. I wasn't very experienced in such things.'

'And I completely misunderstood.'

'And what you said . . . the way you acted . . . I thought I had got it all wrong. You were just having a bit of fun, something to boast about on the site.'

'Oh, Casey. Catherine. My love. How can you ever forgive me for being such a fool?'

She let out a low soft laugh to hear her name in that way on his lips. 'Don't you know, Gil? Don't you know, my darling, how I called myself every kind of fool, and how I waited for you to come back?'

'But Michael . . . ?'

'Michael was a good friend. A loving friend, if you like. But never a lover. I was never able to rid myself of the taste of you, Gil. I told Michael I wouldn't marry him the day after you overheard him in the Bell.'

'And then I barged in with my stupid ultimatum, when all I had to do was tell you that I loved you.'

'That's why I let Dad sell the house. I thought, if I could stop all that, perhaps we could start afresh. When I couldn't, well, I hoped my love would be enough for both of us.'

'Truly, Casey? It was love? Not just the money?'

'If I had wanted to marry money, Gil Blake, I could have been Mrs Michael Hetherington two years ago.' She lowered her lids. 'But perhaps you'd like me to prove it to you?'

'Oh, God, Casey. I love you so much.' He buried his face in her neck, and she sighed as he breathed a trail of kisses down to where the cleft of her breasts was impeded by the silk taffeta. She arched against him as he reached for the zip and slipped the dress down to her waist. For a moment he gazed in wonder at the sight of her bathed in the moonlight filtering through the trees. Then, without haste, he drew one firm nipple into his mouth.

They made love slowly, taking time to enjoy each other, to give and receive an intensity of pleasure that Casey had never, even in her wildest imaginings, dreamt possible. And it was already light when they made their way sleepily back up the hill to Annisgarth.

Gil opened the door and grinned. 'Shall we try it again, Mrs Blake? A new house? A completely new start?'

'Could we? Is it possible?'

His mouth assured her that it was. And then she let out a yell as he swept her off her feet and carried her through into the kitchen.

'Is this a hint?' she asked, laughing.

'Nothing that subtle, woman. I'm starving.' He opened the fridge and pulled out eggs, bacon, a dish of mushrooms and some sausages, which he passed across to Casey.

'It's all stocked up!' she exclaimed, then held up a hand. 'Don't tell me. The totally efficient Darlene.'

He looked hurt. 'Certainly not. I went to the supermarket myself.' He turned back to the fridge. 'This is yours, by the way.' He handed her a long manilla envelope and she opened it curiously, staring at the stiff legal document. It was the deeds to the house. 'You'll have to have it witnessed, then it's all yours.'

She felt the tears suddenly sting the back of her eyes. 'Michael never came here, Gil. I never shared Annisgarth with anyone but you.' She laughed shakily through her tears. 'But, you know, I do believe I'll miss Ladysmith Terrace.'

'Will you?' He kissed her damp cheeks. 'I can't imagine why. But if you want to live there . . . '

'I don't think so. Not because it's . . . '

'A backstreet slum?'

She had the grace to blush. 'No. It's just that, well, it's rather small, and . . . we're going to be needing another bedroom.'

Gil's eyes widened as her meaning sank in. 'A baby?' he breathed. As she nodded, he let out an ecstatic whoop and grabbed her arms. 'We're having a baby?' She nodded, tears of happiness streaming down her face as she was overwhelmed by his excitement. 'Here, sit down.' He pulled out a kitchen chair. 'No. Lie down. Oh, God. You shouldn't have let me . . . not in the damp grass.'

'Gil!' she protested, laughing. 'I'm pregnant, not ill. I'm also very hungry. Please let's cook some breakfast.'

'I'll do it — you rest. Wouldn't you rather lie down?'

'No. I wouldn't.' A tinge of pink coloured her cheeks. 'At least, not until you can lie down with me. We've wasted far too much time already.'

They hadn't wasted any more time in the first year of their marriage, Casey decided, standing beside her husband at the font, their fingers locked together as they watched their daughter receiving her baptismal names.

Held firmly in her godmother's arms, Rose Mary Blake burbled the mildest protest as the vicar poured the holy water over her head. Charlotte clucked soothingly, gazing down at the baby with a besotted expression.

As they walked out into the afternoon sunshine, Gil bent and murmured in his wife's ear, 'Another wedding, very soon, if I'm not mistaken. She's gone all broody.'

Casey giggled. 'Well, babies seem to be in fashion,' she said, as Jennie waddled up to have a look at the infant.

'Do you think she'll make it home before producing?' Gil asked, doubtfully.

'I shouldn't worry about it. It'll be Michael's turn to make the dash to the hospital. And the imminent arrival of a grandchild has certainly turned his mother a good deal sweeter.'

'The course of true love . . . '? Gil murmured.

'Casey!' Charlotte's wail cut through this interesting discussion. 'I think it's time we went. A Rose by any name at all doesn't smell like this.'

'Give her to me,' commanded Mrs O'Connor. 'Grandmothers don't have noses.' And she firmly took control, whisking her away to the nursery as soon as they arrived home, reappearing flushed and with her elegant hat slightly askew, but happy at her first successful tussle with a nappy in more than twenty years.

'She's settled down like a lamb,' she said proudly and Gil solemnly presented his mother-in-law with a glass of champagne.

'You look as if you need this, old darling,' he said, and bent and kissed her cheek, which coloured even more deeply for this attention.

'I'll soon get back my old touch,' she said. 'It's a bit like riding a bicycle. Once you learn, you never forget.'

'You never could ride a bike,' James O'Connor remarked drily, and held out his glass for the offered refill as everyone laughed. 'But you're pretty good at almost everything else.'

'Almost?' his wife demanded indignantly.

'I never could teach you how to poach pheasant.' Gil and Casey exchanged a look and decided without a word that this was a good moment to shepherd their guests through to the dining-room where tea was waiting.

'Michael, could you do the honours with the champagne?' Gil asked. 'I'm sure I heard Rosie crying.' He grabbed Casey's hand and almost ran, from the room.

'Poaching! What kind of family have I married into?' he demanded as he closed the nursery door, and gathered his wife into his arms, shaking with laughter.

Casey nestled against him. 'Do you want your freedom?' she asked, happily.

Gil straightened and looked down at her, suddenly and intensely still. 'Never. Not even in jest.' His lips closed over hers and he kissed her with total dedication until a hiccup from the cot roused him.

★   ★   ★

They were bent over their daughter when the door opened and Charlotte peeped in. 'I thought you'd want to know,' she said, 'that Michael is taking Jennie to the hospital.'

'I told you she'd never make it through the day,' Gil said smugly.

The phone woke Casey in the early hours of the morning. Michael's voice was jubilant as he announced the birth of his son.

'Congratulations. And give Jennie my best wishes. I'll come down and see her.' She hung up and stood there for a moment.

A slight noise behind her made her turn and she smiled as Gil walked up to her, their daughter curled up asleep in the crook of his arm.

'She woke up when the phone rang,' he said, an expression of indescribable gentleness lighting his face, as he gazed down at the sleeping baby.

'Jennie had a boy,' she told him and then tutted. 'Your daughter will be spoilt rotten, Gil Blake, if you pick her up every time she murmurs.' But she couldn't resist touching the tiny curled-up fingers that gripped her even in sleep.

'Thank you, Casey.' She looked up, startled by the intensity in his voice. 'I can't ever remember being so happy.'

'Oh, Gil. I know. I sometimes wake

up in the night and pinch myself to make sure I'm not dreaming.'

'Really?'

'Really.'

He grinned. 'Next time, wake me up. I'll be happy to oblige.'

'Hush,' she laughed. 'You'll wake Rosie.' And, as if she already knew her name, Rose Mary Blake opened her eyes and looked contentedly at her parents.

'Come along, miss. Back to bed with you.' Gil carried her up to the nursery and laid her back in her cot. She opened her mouth to grumble, but fell asleep before any sound came out.

'Pinch me, Gil,' Casey sighed, leaning against the man who had made her so happy.

'With pleasure, my darling. But not here.' He lifted her into his arms, and carried her through to their bedroom. 'Now. Where shall I begin?' he asked.

We do hope that you have enjoyed reading this large print book.

Did you know that all of our titles are available for purchase?

We publish a wide range of high quality large print books including:
Romances, Mysteries, Classics
General Fiction
Non Fiction and Westerns

Special interest titles available in large print are:
The Little Oxford Dictionary
Music Book, Song Book
Hymn Book, Service Book

Also available from us courtesy of Oxford University Press:
Young Readers' Dictionary
(large print edition)
Young Readers' Thesaurus
(large print edition)

For further information or a free brochure, please contact us at:
Ulverscroft Large Print Books Ltd.,
The Green, Bradgate Road, Anstey,
Leicester, LE7 7FU, England.
Tel: (00 44) **0116 236 4325**
Fax: (00 44) **0116 234 0205**

Other titles in the
Linford Romance Library:

THE SANCTUARY

Cara Cooper

City lawyer Kimberley is forced to take over an animal sanctuary left to her in a will. The Sanctuary, a Victorian house overlooking the sea, draws Kimberley under its spell. The same cannot be said for her husband Scott, whose dedication to his work threatens their relationship. When Kimberley comes to the aid of handsome, brooding widower Zach Coen and his troubled daughter, she could possibly help them. But will she risk endangering her marriage in the process?